BLOOD ON THE ROCKS

The ground beneath Kennedy rolled like an ocean swell with flames blazing from the tower's arrow slits and roof. At the peak a tiny figure hovered and plunged downwards ... The tough Glasgow journalist was hitting back — his trail of vengeance blasting a sleepy Scottish island wide open. As gunfire shatters the peace, he fights like a cornered rat. Then, joined by a group of ordinary islanders, Kennedy faces a final fatal battle with a gang of desperate killers.

ARCHIE VENTERS

BLOOD ON THE ROCKS

Complete and Unabridged

LINFORD
Leicester

First published in Great Britain by
Robert Hale Limited
London

First Linford Edition
published 2007
by arrangement with
Robert Hale Limited
London

British Library CIP Data

Venters, Archie
    Blood on the rocks.—Large print ed.—
Linford mystery library
    1. Detective and mystery stories
    2. Large type books
    I. Title
    823.9′14 [F]

    ISBN 978–1–84617–754–5

Published by
F. A. Thorpe (Publishing)
Anstey, Leicestershire

Set by Words & Graphics Ltd.
Anstey, Leicestershire
Printed and bound in Great Britain by
T. J. International Ltd., Padstow, Cornwall

This book is printed on acid-free paper

1

The news reporters of the large Glasgow daily paper shared a long desk. It was littered with typewriters, pools of spilled coffee and tea, discarded stories and empty cigarette-packets. Overflowing typewriter ribbon tins stood in as ashtrays. Thick on the floor like crushed summer flowers were balls of paper containing rejected stories.

Making the head of a T at the end was a smaller desk where the news editor and his deputies surveyed all. The present incumbent was Jack Miller. Fifty and built like a rugby player who had quit the game early to take up golf, he knew within himself that his position was only temporary. News editors had the casualty rate of a Commando assault unit on this newspaper. If ulcers or the booze did not get them, the editor's back-stabbing knife did.

A copy boy threw a first edition in front of him. The black ink was still wet. He snatched it up and leafed through the pages.

'Jesus! It is thin tonight,' he moaned savagely. 'Not one half decent story.'

Kicking back his chair he fled out of the editorial for a reviving whisky.

A couple of reporters held the fort. Old Jock Mitchell was the doyen of the city's press scene. A wizened veteran, he crouched over a radio tuned into the police waveband. The voices of the police operators were cool and detached over the static. The codes were supposed to be secret and changed often, but Jock always managed to obtain a copy before the switch.

Grey eyes yellowed with age studied his companion. David Kennedy was reading through the first edition steadily. Mitchell saw a lean, wiry figure of middle height. A thin angular face topped with straight brown hair cut short — too short in the long-haired eighties. A plain ordinary sort of guy, but for two things.

The old man recalled the colour of his eyes — an unusual sea green. They were as cold as the winter Atlantic. And in a profession where the participants scoffed at sartorial elegance, his neatness in dress was to say the least out of the ordinary.

But Kennedy was a damn good journalist. Mitchell had to admit that. He covered the crime in this city with a history of bloody violence and did it well. Both police and crooks respected and trusted him.

But the old writer was intrigued by him. Where did he come from and what was his background? He had turned up in the city about five years previously and started to freelance. His skill soon got him a staff job. But Mitchell knew no more about him now than he did then.

He let his eyes flick over the reading man again. Late thirties or early forties. Fit and hard. He remembered the last time a mass X-ray unit had visited the newspaper. He had caught a glimpse of Kennedy changing. There were a couple of puckered scars on his back and chest. Mitchell had last seen them when he had been fighting his war to end all wars . . . bullet scars!

Now where had Kennedy picked up

those souvenirs? He had never mentioned Army service.

Kennedy read on unaware of the old man's scrutiny. Usually he was sensitive to such close examination. In the past, his very life had hung on the realization of being watched. But this evening he was depressed and withdrawn.

He rose and crossed to the large window overlooking the street below already bustling with delivery vans. Late summer, daylight still lingered. Light rain whispered down and covered the glass like fine oil.

His eyes hardened as he thought of the city out there. A million ordinary folk doing ordinary things. But as the darkness crept stealthily over the roofs, the evil ones slithered out like rats on the hunt. He wondered what violence was being plotted out there. Those who denied the laws of God and man thrived in the night.

The city had had more than its share of violent crime recently. Not stupid, senseless felonies by mindless hoodlums, but well planned bank raids and payroll holdups. Guns had been used freely and a lot of innocent people had ended up very dead.

His frown deepened. It was the same story all over the United Kingdom. The raids were carried out with all the skill of military operations. The criminals hit fast and then vanished. No matter how swiftly road-blocks and the like were organized the gunmen disappeared into thin air.

A phone behind disturbed his gloomy thoughts. A deep voice growled, 'Alex Houston here. Any chance of seeing you tonight?'

Houston was a Detective Chief Inspector on the Regional Crime Squad. Tough, resourceful and a fund of good copy. They made arrangements to meet later in a south-side pub.

The policeman did not say what it was about, but few cops talked business over a telephone.

They had become acquainted during a particularly nasty teenage-girl killing. It resulted in a close friendship. The newspaperman had also introduced the big detective to the girl he was now engaged to. He had met Margaret Anderson at a cocktail party and taken her out a couple of times. She was a tall willowy girl just the right side of thirty. Her hair was waist-long and black as the pit. Keen blue eyes danced in an elfin face. Extremely intelligent, she was the private secretary to one of the most important financial figures in Scotland.

But there had been nothing between them. He had been honestly happy when Margaret and Alex had paired off. He was infatuated with her and she accepted him with a contented tolerance.

He was just bending to get into his car — an immaculate 1951 MG sports that he doted on — a few minutes later, when the front door porter cried his name. He was wanted on the phone again.

'David, have you heard from Alex?' It was Margaret. Her voice betrayed worry.

'Aye. Only a few minutes ago. I am just going down to police headquarters and will be meeting him later for a drink. You two have a fight or something?'

'No, but he dropped in to see me earlier and he just was not himself. I am sure he had something serious on his mind. He has been working too hard lately. Oh blast, I expect I am just being silly.'

'I wouldn't let it get you down too much,' said Kennedy softly. 'He has a lot on his plate at the moment with these big robberies. I'll get him to give you a tinkle later.'

Over an hour passed before he set out for the meeting. Except for a couple of minor traffic accidents the city was quiet.

The MG purred through a desolate wasteland of broken-down and abandoned buildings. Few lights glimmered in the high tenements. Smashed windows were like dead men's eye sockets.

He parked the car beneath a lone street light that somehow had escaped the vandals. The pub was burrowed into the foot of a high empty tenement. Why had Alex selected this dump? Maybe the detective did not want to be seen with him for some reason.

Pushing aside the old-fashioned swing doors — very handy when ejecting troublesome customers — he stepped inside. One room with the bar running down the wall on the left. There was only one other door, marked 'Gents'. It was very doubtful if a gentleman had ever passed through it. The bare wooden floor was blackened by countless cigarettes being ground into it. A coal fire glowing in a tiny grate did little to combat the dampness in the air. There was a heavy smell made up of a mixture of whisky, beer, vomit, urine and tobacco.

A dozen or so men stood about chatting and drinking with that religious fervour Scots give to alcohol. One or two faces turned in his direction, then slid away.

He weaved through them to the bar, careful not to look at anyone directly. A straight stare in this type of drinking-establishment could end up with blood being spilled . . . his!

The whisky was surprisingly good. Its warmth loosened muscles stiff with cold and dampness. The only barman had the hands of an efficient slaughterman. His sly eyes flicked constantly around the room searching for the first signs of trouble.

Kennedy let himself slip into the anonymity that was as part of the place as the bottles behind the bar. A mean joint in every way, he still felt comfortable there. No ulcerated management types were here trying to forget the tensions of their mad world of commerce. No worried husbands kept glancing over their shoulders as they chatted up their secretaries.

The customers about him were just out to get as drunk as possible — as quickly as possible. The conversation was just as straightforward — football, horses and dogs. They were mainly small scrawny men, but with the wiry strength of gutsy mongrels.

The front door swung shut with a bang. Alex had arrived. A hush came down like shutters over the bar. A few turned away swiftly. Others became terribly interested in the bottom of their glasses. One man slipped into the toilet and most probably out of the window.

These lads could smell a copper.

Houston was built like the side of a double-decker bus. He had a square aggressive face. His nose was bent round towards his right ear. The result of a bloke resisting arrest. The detective had put him in hospital for six weeks.

Tonight his lips were tight and bright blue eyes clouded. He spotted the journalist and strutted heavily to the bar and grunted a dour greeting.

Kennedy ordered another two whiskies. The barman placed them down and retired to the other end of the varnished counter where he polished glasses with unexpected energy.

The policeman hunched over his drink. Kennedy could sense an anger in him, but waited in silence.

Finally the big man spoke. 'How are things?'

'Fair to hellish,' replied Kennedy lightly. 'Haven't seen you about recently. I heard you were out of town.'

The intense face turned. No-one was within earshot. The other drinkers had drifted away and were giving them plenty of elbow-room.

'Aye. I was up at George Campbell's funeral.' There was a harshness in the reply that jolted the reporter.

Sergeant Campbell had been a long-server in the police in the city. A soft-spoken Highlander with impeccable manners, even when dealing with falling-down drunks. He had been a native of the Isle of Bargrennan. One of a thousand islands off the west coast, but larger than most. He had drowned in a boating accident when on holiday there recently. He had written a short obituary for the paper.

'Why did you go up?'

'George was a bachelor with no close relatives. Someone on the Force had to attend and I volunteered. I was on the beat with him just after I joined and he taught me a lot that they have never heard of at Police College. He was a good copper.'

Houston raised his glass as if toasting the dead man's memory. Maybe he was.

'You were away for a long time just for a funeral,' commented Kennedy thoughtfully.

'George had been fishing on the loch just off the castle when the accident must have occurred. The local lads carried out an investigation, but were satisfied it was an accident. These things happen all the time. A dizzy turn, a stumble and in they go.

'But something niggled me. There was a smell about it. I just had a feeling. So I took a few days off and did a bit of digging.'

Kennedy dropped his cigarette and heeled it out. 'Find anything?'

'Damn all! But I've still got that feeling.'

Houston did not elaborate about his stay at Bargrennan. Kennedy changed the subject.

'Getting anywhere with these raids?'

The detective cursed and hit the bar with his fist. No-one turned round. 'Every copper in the country is working on them. But we have come up with nothing. But I'd bet my pension there is one well organized mob behind them all.

'Each raid is identical. Get in fast, cut down anyone in sight and then vanish.'

They discussed the heists for a short time and then Kennedy recalled the girl's call.

'By the way, have you and Margaret had a fight?'

Unexpected hostility in Houston's eyes made him flinch.

'What gave you that idea?' snarled the policeman.

'She got in touch with me at the office a little while ago. She was concerned about you and thought the work might be getting on top of you. I said I would get you to call her.'

The detective shook himself. 'Forget what she thinks. There are a couple of questions I want to ask you, David. That is why I asked you to meet me tonight.'

'Fire away, Alex. What is it all about?'

Houston's strong hands were clenched in tight fists. Something was eating away at his guts.

The background buzz that had covered their own voices fell away like a foaming wave down a beach. A youngster in his early twenties stood uneasily at the door. Frowning, he nodded Houston over.

For the first time a smile crossed the big man's face. 'He is with me. I don't think that he approves of our meeting here. Still believes a copper should not drink on duty. He has not found out yet that it is the only thing that keeps us sane.

'Something must have come up on the car radio. Hang on here a minute.'

The whole bar watched out of the side of their eyes as the heavy figure strode out.

A sigh welled up to be cut short by two quite separate whiplash cracks. The doors swung back very, very slowly. They were being forced open by Houston's broad shoulders. In slow motion he fell backwards to the dirty floor like a felled tree. His head struck the wood with a sodden thump.

Kennedy shuddered. His news editor would have his decent story now. He had just witnessed a cop killing!

2

All hell broke out. Glasses were dropped and beer swilled across the floor. Someone shouted something about the IRA.

Four steps and Kennedy was on his knees beside his friend. Two black-edged holes marred the white shirt. Red blood gurgled up out of them in spurts.

Shock was etched on Houston's face. The skin was already sagging back on the bones of his skull. His lips were drawn back over his yellowish teeth. The blue eyes were bulging. Their brightness was beginning to dull as his hold on life slackened.

Kennedy gripped the limp hand fiercely as if he could prevent the doomed man slipping over the edge of eternity. Houston's lips moved. He bent low over him.

Blood flowed through the clenched teeth and down his chin. He was trying to speak but the blood choked his efforts.

Kennedy squeezed the hand hard and held his eyes with his.

The detective suddenly raised himself on one elbow. His throat muscles stood out like straining wires as he tried to stop the rising flood gushing from his mouth.

'Get Margaret.' It was only a light fluttering of breath. His face twisted into a hideous mask of agony. He shuddered and fell back. A final spout of blood burst from his mouth and fell away as if a tap had been turned off.

All his life Kennedy had flirted with violent death . . . all those years in the Marines, a spell with the Aussies in Vietnam and as a journalist. Friends had died before, but he could never get used to it. Each time a fragment of his own soul withered.

Raising his head he found the other drinkers standing silently. One old fellow had removed his cloth cap. Kennedy went to speak but another burst of gunfire cut him off short. Splinters of wood and diamond-bright slivers of glass showered down as lead tore through the door and windows.

Kennedy scrambled wildly to the wall. He edged the door ajar but could see nothing. Another rattle of fire made him flinch, but this time the pub was not the target.

A cold fury suddenly possessed him. His nerves were steady, but his stomach seemed filled with iced water.

'Throw that chair through the window,' he rasped at the nearest prostrate figure.

The little man had the sinewy look of an engineer about him. But although now collecting his old-age pension he was still as hard as the steel he used to work with.

Taking a firm grip of the chair he grinned happily. 'The last time I did something like this I got fourteen days in nick.' With that he hurled the chair through the glass.

The reporter leapt forward like a sprinter and took the swing doors with his shoulders. He skidded uncontrollably across the slimy pavement to smash into the police car. Dropping, he wriggled desperately to the rear wheel.

The young policeman was kneeling at the front door. Kennedy screamed at him to get behind the engine. Bullets would whip through the thin bodywork like butter. The engine block would give him some protection.

Opposite stood one of the abandoned tenements awaiting the demolishers.

Flashes of eye-searing light heralded a hail of bullets across the vehicle. He hugged the wheel like a lover. The car took on a list like a sinking ship as the offside wheels were shredded. Window glass sprinkled over his hair like frozen snow. The car's second-hand value was dropping fast.

The shots were coming from the covering darkness of an entrance right opposite. The gunman was invisible.

'Alex is dead!' he shouted. 'Have you radioed for assistance?'

The policeman nodded without turning his head.

'Then there is nothing we can do here. That bastard has us pinned down. After the next burst get into the pub and we will wait for your mates.'

He doubted if the killer would follow. With each passing second he would be thinking more and more of escape.

The detective's fresh face was ashen with fear and tension. He did not look young any longer. Kennedy guessed what was churning about inside the lad's head.

'Don't be a bloody fool!' he yelled fervently. 'Wait.'

Shaking his head, the detective jumped to his feet and raced over the rain-streaked road. His long legs went like pistons. His right hand clutched his pathetic truncheon like a relay baton.

For a moment it seemed as if the lad was going to make it. But a string of hammering slugs reached out and stitched down his chest and stomach. The slim victim was lifted into the air and flung backwards to collapse like a bundle of dirty rags.

Kennedy risked a glance round the side of the car. The killer had got both policemen and would now want to make his break for freedom. Bullets whipped past his cheek.

His lungs emptied in a scream of terror. The gunman was after him as well! The thought was unbelievable. Cops got shot — but never reporters. What the hell was he going to do?

The bar offered some measure of security. Bracing himself he jumped for the door — and bounced off the firm wood. It was locked! He hammered despairingly until a burst of fire nearly took his hands off at the wrists.

Back behind his friendly wheel again, a raw resentment replaced the alarm that had threatened to overwhelm him. He was tired of being a target.

The street was wrapped in silence. Then he heard some sharp metallic clicks. The killer was changing magazines and seemed to be having some difficulty.

Dragging in a deep breath, Kennedy flung himself for the other side of the street. He ran at an angle out of the direct line of fire. The wind of bullets fluttering over his left shoulder added impetus to his lunging legs. The last ten feet to the shelter of an adjacent entrance he took in one crazy leap.

Leaning against the wall he found cold sweat streaming from his body. He could hear police sirens some streets away. So would the gunman. They would force him to take off and vanish into the maze of surrounding derelict buildings.

Kennedy slipped through the dark tunnel of the entrance to the back court beyond. It was a deep pool of shifting shadows. Carefully he slid along the wall.

Snail-like he edged into the passageway that hid the killer and was swallowed up in Stygian darkness. Shutting his eyes he strained to pick up the slithering of shoes over the damp flagstones. Or the quick breathing of a desperate man. Nothing!

The wall was dank and sticky beneath his fingers. The rustle of the cloth of his trousers rubbing together, his breathing and the pumping of his heart combined to fill the air with noise.

The front entrance showed as a rectangular shape. There was no-one there. He had to turn a bend to reach the stairs. Maybe he was there, gun levelled and finger on the trigger.

Swallowing the hard lump that blocked his throat, he eased round the corner — ready to jump back at the first sound — even though he knew it would be too late. Nine-millimetre slugs travel fast. A lot faster than he could scuttle back.

A little light filtered in from the street. He ran his eyes up the stairs and felt his muscles seize. The dark purple shadow of a man was huddled near the top.

A hoarse whisper reached down to him. 'It wis'nae me, mister. The man wi' the gun is upstairs. I'm comin' doon. Don't hit me, mister.'

His shoulders slumped with relief. 'Okay. Slowly with your hands up. I have a gun and as much as cough and your brains will redecorate the wall,' he lied softly.

The figure sidled down like a whipped dog and Kennedy slammed him back against the wall. A belch of foul breath hit him full in the face and made him gag — a wino! One of the lost tribe of alcoholics who haunted these empty places.

'Honest, I wis only having a wee drink upstairs when the shootin' started, mister,' he stuttered. 'I came doon aboot a minute ago. The man wi' the gun ran back, but he did'nae seem to ken the way oot the back and went up the stairs — right past me. He went into one of the hooses on the first floor.

'And that's the honest truth, mister.'

The journalist pushed the pathetic figure away from him. The wino could be telling the truth — most probably was. A stranger to a tenement could very easily go astray.

He started warily up the narrow stairs. Old newspapers crunched beneath his shoes. His groping fingers wrapped round a bottle that sloshed. The wino must really have been scared stiff to have left that. Holding it like a club, he went on climbing.

A door to a flat hung open on the first landing. He peered in. Two doors faced him. His quarry would be in there somewhere and most probably in the room on the right where he could watch any activity in the street below.

He lowered himself to the hall floor and pulled himself across the cracked linoleum to the door. A board creaked under his elbow and the click of a gun bolt sounded clearly. The sod was definitely in there!

He rested his wet forehead on the linoleum. What next? He did not waste time thinking of what he could have done with a rifle and grenade. It was his wits against a sub-machine-gun. He had to make do with what he had.

The bottle! Pulling out the cork, he sniffed — the surgical clean smell of methylated spirits. Poor old bastard.

He poured a little on to his handkerchief and stuffed it into the neck of the bottle. Kneeling at one side of the door, he got out his lighter. It was a chance in a thousand — but still a chance. Would his lighter flash first time? His life depended on its doing just that!

Turning the handle, he flung the door back. Streaks of scarlet lightning accompanied by a chattering chorus of thunder burst out above him. He flicked the lighter's wheel. Thank God, it lit! He touched the flame to the meths soaked linen which immediately blazed up.

The shots had come from the centre of the room. With a strong flick of his wrist, he cast the bottle in as another burst sought him out. The makeshift Molotov cocktail blew up with a shattering explosion. High-pitched screams like those of a dying rabbit rose from within.

The gunman was a mass of flames — blue dancing flames. They flickered over his hair and clothes. He was trying to beat out his own funeral pyre with blackened hands.

But the murderer had guts. The machine-gun lay at his feet where he had dropped it when the world had blown up in his face. He snatched it up with fumbling fingers and tried to train it on Kennedy. The hellish fire-shrouded figure was intent on taking his tormentor with him.

Kennedy jerked himself out of a horrified trance and dived forward. His hunched shoulder drove into the burning man's gut. Fire stung his face and neck. Staggering back, the killer gave a final wail and fell out of the smashed open window. There was a soggy thump and the keening ceased.

Both hands on the sill, the reporter looked down. His victim was an untidy crumpled heap on the pavement.

Two white police cars with blue lights flashing were parked outside the pub. Blue-uniformed figures cautiously approached the cremated cop-killer. A few men ventured out of the bar. Some still clutched glasses. One walked over and poured his pint over the flames. Kennedy heard the hissing and threw up.

Kennedy was fuming and, free from fear, his anger was all the greater. His fingernails gouged into the thick varnish that coated the desk of Detective Chief Superintendent Angus Macdonald. For over two hours he had been held at the police office.

He tried to keep his voice under control, but it still shook. 'I want to phone my paper now! That sergeant has my statement but will not let me get to a phone. On your orders, he claimed. My news editor will be going out of his tiny skull. Now either I use a phone or all hell is going to break out in here.'

Macdonald had come down from the Isle of Skye in the early fifties to join the Force. His family had hoped that the young islander would have become a minister in the Free Kirk. But that much-respected body that was the self-designated keeper of the Skye folks' morals had discovered that Angus was partial to the odd dram. And that was that. Like many a young Highlander before him that left only one thing — the Glasgow Police. It was the Skye equivalent of joining the Foreign Legion.

The senior officer's bland expression did not alter, but the soft brown eyes hardened. 'I have just had two men shot down in cold blood. Now just you sit there and do what you are told or I will go out of my tiny skull. You will get in touch with your paper when I tell you and not before.'

The soft voice disguised a terrible anger and fury of emotion. The younger man realized he was acting like a petulant schoolboy and fell back into a chair.

'Sorry. I'm just tired. I have had enough for one night.'

'Now, David, tell me what happened out there.' The Highland accent was more pronounced.

Kennedy protested that it was all in his statement. But Macdonald insisted that he hear it for himself. There might be some minor detail seemingly not important that might just interest him.

The reporter talked for twenty minutes. His profession had also given him an eye for detail and he neglected nothing. Macdonald sat in silence, hands folded on a spotless white blotter. Pinpoints of light flashed in his eyes as his computer-like brain went over the information fed into it. Items were filed away and indexed in the grey cell matter. Each item had its place. Nothing was cast aside as useless.

'Has he been identified?' finished Kennedy.

Macdonald shook his head. The fact that his face was ruined was not going to help either.

'You have no idea yourself why my men were murdered?'

The seated reporter shrugged.

'And Alex did not go into what he was working on at the moment?'

'No. We chatted mainly about George Campbell's accident and that he was not happy about the accident theory. That and the fact that no-one was getting anywhere on those big raids.'

Macdonald murmured that he had been aware of Houston's feelings on Campbell's death. He had dropped in the day before to report on his trip to Bargrennan. It had been an unsatisfactory meeting.

He had told the dead detective to drop it. The police up north had been satisfied that it had been an unfortunate accident. Then Houston had confessed that he had a theory on the big raids that needed checking out. The senior officer had tried to press him on it.

'But he insisted that his theory would sound too fantastic. There were facts he would have to look into. The funny thing was that he did not seem very excited over it — rather the opposite, in fact.'

The phone rang. Macdonald apologized and lifted the receiver with a huge hand covered in black hair. He listened for some minutes and then replaced it without comment.

'I sent a policewoman over to break the

bad news to Alex's fiancée. That was her reporting in. The lassie took it well — what a horrible expression that is, don't you think? Breaking her heart inside most likely. My girl will stay with her tonight.'

He went on to say that they were sure the slaying was not the work of any terrorist group. They usually got in touch with one of the press agencies and claimed responsibility for anything of that sort. This time they were silent. But he was hoping the forensic boys would come up with something from the corpse within the next twenty-four hours.

Kennedy began to worry about his newspaper again. A swift glance at his watch showed he would still be able to make the final edition.

Little lines appeared around the gruff policeman's eyes. 'I am afraid your story will not be used. There will not even be a mention that you were involved. The story being carried by all the papers — with the agreement of the editors — is that two policemen were murdered by a gunman. He died as the result of an explosive device he was carrying going up acciden-tally.'

Kennedy felt the blood drain from his face. His previous rage swept over him like a tidal wave. He bit his lip and clenched his fists. His nerves had taken a thrashing that night and he had to stay cool.

'Don't give me that!' he almost yelled. 'My editor would never stand for the paper being gagged like this. You'll end up crucified!'

'Now calm down,' murmured Mac-donald placatingly. 'I am thinking of your safety. I am sure that whoever planned this massacre was just after my own men. The poor devil who fried was just his instrument.

'But why were they killed? Could it have been that Alex had really stumbled over a lead in connection with these raids?'

The detective got up and walked up and down his office for a few moments. 'At the moment I am working in the dark. But I am pretty certain that you were the typical innocent bystander. Maybe he thought you were another cop.

'But one thing is for certain — I want to make sure that the man who issued the orders for those killings never hears of your part in it. You might just be asked to play a return match . . . and this time not be so lucky. That is why you are being kept out of it.'

Kennedy mumbled that he could understand Macdonald's concern. But insisted his boss would never stand for such censorship.

'My news editor wouldn't care if I was hung, drawn and quartered before an audience of thousands at Hampden Park — as long as I got the story in first.'

'I got that opinion myself,' retorted Macdonald with a smile. 'Miller, isn't it. He was a wee bit annoyed about my suggestion. But Sir Colin agreed with me and that was that. You see Sir Colin and I are old friends. We came down from Skye together, you know.'

The journalist shook his head in disbelief. Sir Colin Forbes was the owner of the newspaper — and many more besides. He allowed himself to be guided by the elbow to the door. Sir Colin had passed on an order that he had to go straight home to bed.

His home was a small flat in the city's west end. It was fairly Spartan, but clean and comfortable.

It was a long time before he went to sleep. And when he finally did nightmares of blood and fire twisted through his restless mind.

3

Margaret lived in a small square. She led him into the sitting-room of the terrace house. It was a large room where warm velvet coverings were predominant. Glass, crystal and china ornaments teetered on the mantelpiece, shelves and delicate tables. Strange exotic plants filled the air with a cloying scent.

Her long black hair hung loose. A simple black dress emphasized her slimness. The early-morning sun through the windows accentuated the whiteness of her skin.

For a moment she seemed about to speak, but instead stumbled into his arms. Deep sobs racked her body cruelly. He held her gently as he would a sick child. Gradually her weeping ceased and the shaking shoulders stilled. He guided her to a chair.

Clutching a sodden wisp of white lace, her face mirrored broken hopes and dashed dreams. 'Why, David?' she moaned.

He rubbed a hand over his eyes. 'No-one knows. The CID are working on it but I don't think they are getting anywhere. I am afraid they will want to talk to you.' He reached over and touched her fingers. 'I was with him when he died. He did not suffer. Right at the end he wanted you with him.'

The stricken girl raised her head and a new light flickered at the back of her eyes. 'He asked for me?'

He nodded slowly.

A little colour seeped back into her cheeks. Standing up, she shook out her hair. Slim fingers smoothed out her dress. Did he want a drink? She poured two very dry sherries into fragile crystal glasses.

In a flat but firm tone she asked him to recount how her fiancé had died. Every detail. He protested uselessly. Avoiding her gaze he recounted the bloody episode.

'So you avenged him!' There was a cruel shine in her eyes that he did not like to see there.

The doorbell rang and she excused

herself. He tried to light a cigarette with a shaking hand, but the flint of his lighter had gone. If that had happened a few hours previously he would now have been taking up space at the mortuary. He picked up a book of matches from a china ashtray.

Margaret returned. It had been a neighbour offering sympathy.

'I have got to go anyway,' he said gently. 'Now if there is anything you need, get in touch. Even if you just want someone to chat to.'

The whole top floor of the newspaper building was occupied by the owner. There was living accommodation and a number of offices. Sir Colin Forbes had many business interests and held the reins of his empire from up there.

His own office resembled the reading-room of one of the better London clubs. All brown leather and beeswaxed wood. He had no desk, but did all his paperwork at a fine antique table. Dark paintings of gloomy Scottish mountains and rampant stags hung from the panelled walls. Queen Victoria would have approved of the decor.

The proprietor already had company — editor George Nicolson, a dried-up, emaciated man never known to smile.

Sir Colin lumbered across the room on thick, slightly bowed legs. A huge hand swallowed the reporter's without trace. For some reason Kennedy was surprised at the strength in the grip.

'That was a terrible experience last night. But you did well, very well.'

There was no trace of the mountain boy left in his accent. But until he opened his mouth, the bulky man could have been mistaken for a hill farmer down for a day in the big city. His shoulders strained at the stitching of a thick tweed suit.

'Thank you, sir. But I still wish I had been allowed to write my own story.'

Black eyes under bushy eyebrows gleamed with irritation for a second, then cleared. 'For your own good, Kennedy. Your very life might have been at risk if we had publicized the depth of your involvement.' He let loose a burst of laughter. 'And I doubt if the lawyers would ever have allowed it. Now come and have a drink.'

He offered his employees a glass of some obscure malt whisky from his home island. 'Never drink anything else myself. It is magnificent.'

Sir Colin sipped his with obvious relish. Kennedy covered a grimace. It tasted like French polish. Irreverently he thought the boss must have obtained it from some of his bare-shanked cousins with a hidden still in the high mountains.

'Definitely superb, sir!' Nicolson was never one to miss a chance.

The owner waved them to deep armchairs. 'Some day you will be able to write the full story. That will be the day that the killers are sentenced. Until then you stay quiet. Have you any theories on the matter?'

Kennedy hesitated and Sir Colin's eyes flashed impatiently.

'Well, sir, for various reasons I think that an organization was behind this killing. If it had not been for that sub-machine gun I might just have accepted the loner with a grudge theory. But a weapon that sophisticated would be unavailable to him.'

Nicolson snorted over his glass. 'Rubbish! I know we are still not as bad as the States, but guns of all types are on the increase amongst the crooks in this country.'

'But that one used last night was an American Ingram — one of the most sophisticated models in the world. No ordinary Glasgow ned could get one. And remember cop killings are still not common in this country. Usually a policeman dies only when a crook panics and pulls the tit. This one was planned.'

He went on to explain that Houston had thought he might be on to something pertaining to the big raids. Maybe he had come across something, a real big lead, and that was why he was silenced.

'And what are your own thoughts on these robberies?' boomed Sir Colin topping up their glasses with the amber liquid fire.

The reporter was silent for a time as he considered his answer. Glasgow was the home of some of the most efficient and vicious mobs in the country. He had contacts within them. And they were as mystified as the law agencies. Whoever was knocking over the banks and payrolls, it was not a regular gang. It was the same story in the other big cities.

'I believe they are being carried out by a new group with no criminal records. Amateurs, in fact.'

'Ridiculous!' scoffed Nicolson sneeringly. 'The planning for each raid was superb. Their intelligence network is first-class. They always hit the right place at the right time. And they are utterly ruthless. Does that sound like a bunch of amateurs?'

'And why not, man?' cut in Sir Colin quickly. 'The Great Train Robbers were amateurs and look what they got away with! This could be why the investigating officers are having so much difficulty. Kennedy, you may have something here. Go on.'

The reporter had little to add. Except that witnesses were shot out of hand. Real professionals planned to avoid killings. Bodies only meant a bigger and more intense hunt. If he was right this new group killed wantonly, then vanished to become nice ordinary citizens again.

It was all pure supposition. He did not have one real fact to go on, but it would explain a lot.

'I like it, Kennedy,' conceded the owner. 'Yes, I like it. From now on you are off your routine job. I want you to follow up this line. Try and find out if Houston was really on to something. You knew the man and the way he worked and thought. If it exists find this organization.'

Kennedy carefully placed his empty glass on the arm of his chair. He was dumbfounded. The man did not realize what he was asking!

'That would be a waste of time, sir.' Sir Colin flushed angrily but he rushed on. 'If the police are drawing a blank with their facilities and skills, how can I hope to succeed? And I am sure they will have thought of this angle as well.'

Sir Colin Forbes smiled. It did not reach his eyes. 'You are quite right. They are professionals. But it might need an amateur to catch amateurs. Get to it.'

Kennedy found himself on the street

outside. What a bloody assignment! He supposed that like a good private eye he should head for a bar and four fingers of rye. Where the hell was he going to start?

The morning clouds had rushed on to their final destination somewhere over the northern mountains. A hot sun reflected brightly from the granite pavements. Clerks, tradesmen, schoolchildren and shop assistants swarmed out into the glorious sunlight.

Kennedy felt his step lighten and spirits rise as the mood caught him. Strolling along, hands in his pockets, he watched the light breeze whip and snatch at summer dresses and admired shapely legs. He found that he was hungry. The sun called for an Italian meal and a bottle of Chianti. The very place was just a few streets away.

The laughing, jostling crowd carried him along. Bumping went unheeded. The press of happy faces stopped at a crossing. Traffic thundered by. He watched for the lights to change.

Suddenly a hand hit him in the small of the back. As he shot forward a foot hooked his ankle and he went sprawling. Shrill screams shattered the shock that paralysed his muscles. A huge container lorry was hurtling down on him. He caught a glimpse of the driver's horrified face as he leaned backwards forcing down the brake pedal. Then the bonnet cut out the sky. The engine roaring filled his ears.

His body lay right across its path. If one giant wheel missed, the other would grind him to pulp. His fingernails tore at the tarmac. With a scream he rolled into the foetus position as if trying to return to the safety of the womb.

The blackness of death reached out over him. He was falling and twisting into a bottomless pool. Then there was nothing.

* * *

'I was not knocked unconscious,' snarled Kennedy at Chief Superintendent Macdonald. 'I bloody well fainted with fright. I thought I was about to be smeared all over the damned road. It was lucky for me that the bastard pushed me under a container lorry — plenty of clearance underneath. If it had been a car or bus . . . '

He was back in the detective's office. His face and hands were criss-crossed with scratches nipping like fury from whatever that damned nurse at the hospital had put on them.

'Someone is really determined to get rid of me!'

Macdonald smiled reassuringly. 'Don't let your imagination run away with you, laddie. That sort of accident happens all the time. There were a lot of people around you. Many in a hurry. One unfortunately bumped into you. I doubt if they were even aware of it.'

'It was no accidental bump. I was shoved and tripped.'

The detective explained a traffic warden had arrived on the scene only seconds after the accident. He had questioned some youngsters who had witnessed his nose dive on to the road. No-one had seen him pushed. He was still a bit uptight over the previous night.

'Oh, what the hell!' sighed the news-paperman. He could never convince Macdonald that the push had been deliberate. Had anything been found out about the dead man?

'Damn little!' No identification on him. His fingerprints were not on record. His clothes were all brand-new from one of the big multiples.

But the first report from the scientific types was interesting. The gunman had been in his early twenties and fit. But had gained that fitness from sport and not hard manual work. He had spent a lot of time in the open air — could have been an athlete. His hands were more suited to a golf club than a machine-gun.

'They have just started cutting the young bastard up and may come up with more. But it is their opinion that he came from a good upper-middle-class back-ground. Now what was a lad like that doing shooting up two police officers? It makes no sense.'

Kennedy's heart quickened and he forgot his aches and pains. The descrip-tion did not add up to the usual hoodlum and he recalled the killer had got lost in a tenement.

On the desk was spread what looked like the usual contents of any man's pockets. Some cash, comb, cigarettes, lighter, notebook, pen, knife, cheque-book, other documents and a book of matches.

'Alex's?'

Macdonald nodded grimly and drummed his fingers on the desk top.

'Tell you anything?'

A negative shake.

He reached out and lifted the lighter. It burst into flame at the first flick.

Macdonald drew a clip-board from a drawer. 'His car log sheet. Have a look at it.'

The familiar neat writing showed the trips of that last shift. Not many and they ceased after he had noted Margaret's address.

'There is a gap of about two hours from the time he left Margaret's place until he met me,' he observed uneasily. 'Where did he get to?'

The older man shrugged. He had no

idea. The missing trip or trips were a mystery. He had not called in on any of the city police offices. That had been checked out.

An hour later Kennedy parked his MG outside a small factory on the banks of the Clyde. It stood almost alone amongst other dirty buildings and crumbling warehouses.

The manager resembled one of his own products — a thin body topped by a completely round red face. His hair was the colour of freshly scrubbed carrots.

Standing at the window of his office, he pointed at the river. 'Right up to the war our timber was brought right up to the factory by barge. It is surprising how much wood a match factory requires.

'But how can I help you, Mr Kennedy?'

The journalist had palmed the book of matches from Macdonald's desk. He could always return it later with the excuse that he had put it in his pocket by mistake. He looked at it once again before handing it over to the manager. The plain glossy red cover was still shining and unscratched. No matches had been used from it. It could only have been in Alex's pocket for a short time.

'Can you tell me who this was made for, Mr Watson?'

The match-manufacturer examined it closely. 'A nice piece of work. I would guess it is a give-away. You know the sort of thing. You get them in some hotels and bars. But why are you so interested?'

The newspaperman explained that it might help his inquiries on a murder story. Watson got visibly excited.

'Will my name appear in the paper?' His small eyes glowed.

Kennedy felt like wringing his scrawny neck. He swallowed hard. It was an effort to keep the contempt from his voice. 'Of course, if your information proves valuable.'

'Well we did not make it. We only do boxes, but I have an idea who did. Excuse me for a moment.'

It took two phone calls to track down the maker.

'Right, Mr Kennedy, I have got what you wanted. It was a special order for a gambling-establishment right here in

Glasgow — the Club Scarlet.'

Driving back into the city centre Kennedy went over what he knew about the gambling-club. It had been open for a couple of years and from the first had been a success. A fortune had been spent in creating it and it brought in a fortune. It offered its members excellent cuisine, fine wines and an international cabaret and the gambling was honest.

The membership list read like a Scottish 'Who's Who'.

The manager was a very smooth American. Bernie McGuire could have stepped right off a Mississippi gambling-boat of the last century. He reminded him of a young Douglas Fairbanks Jnr.

Kennedy knew him passably well. He had covered the opening and given it a well-deserved write-up. The following morning a membership card had been dropped in at the office. He used it now and then when he wanted to impress. He had cracked a bottle with McGuire more than once. And was aware that under the well-cut dinner-suit lurked a very hard man indeed.

But how had Alex come by that book of matches? It had only been in his pocket for a short time. Could he have spent that missing time in the club? If so — why?

There was only one way to find out. A call to Margaret found her a little better, but she did not feel like dining at the Club Scarlet that evening.

4

Kennedy nodded to the doorman as he entered the club. His rate of progress slowed as the thick carpet clutched at his shoes. He wallowed over to the Adams-type staircase that curved up to the restaurant and bars. A dolly in a tight silk dress wiggled up ahead of him. The two small protuberances of her bottom rolled and swayed delightfully as if they had a life all of their own.

The restaurant was deliberately garish — it could have been the set for a 1940 movie. The tables were close and the music low.

The bar was on a platform above the level of the diners. He wrapped his legs round a tall stool and ordered a large Black Label. Below there were quite a few familiar faces — businessmen, television personalities, idle rich and some were even accompanied by their wives.

He had a nodding acquaintance with

the barman — a slim, golden-haired youth who wore a little make-up. 'The boss about?'

Long black eyelashes fluttered. 'Mr McGuire is upstairs in the casino.'

It would be a waste of time asking the nancy-boy if he had seen Houston the previous evening. The club staff were all members of the Three Brass Monkeys' Union. And the members paid high for that discretion.

The casino was no modern chrome and steel Las Vegas joint. The air vibrating with the solid clunk of one-armed bandits. The cries of winners and moans of the unfortunate. Where everything is designed to separate the mugs from their cash as swiftly as possible. Here the object was to make them hand it over with quiet dignity.

He stopped at the entrance to let his eyesight adjust. At first he could see little in the dark purple atmosphere like the deep shades of a late evening. Slowly his vision improved and he could pick out tables, the gamblers only silhouettes against thin beams from overhead lights.

Only their hooked fingers nervously tapping the green baize could be seen clearly.

Thick wine-red drapes cut out the rude sound of the normal world outside. A carpet that could have given cover to a hunted fox deadened his footsteps as he drifted from game to game.

He was watching a roulette wheel, the tiny ball clattering and jumping, when he sensed a figure behind him. Turning, he found a heavyweight hovering over him. The face above the neat black bow tie was hidden in the shadow, but the eyes glowed cruelly.

'Mr McGuire asked if you would join him.' It was no request but an order. Sometime he had taken a chop on the throat and the message came out in a croaking rasp.

The gambler had a private room at one end of the casino. It was not an office. That was downstairs. This was more a place for private entertaining. It was definitely masculine. Deep comfortable chairs with small side tables for glasses. A writing-table against one wall. In the centre was a green leather-topped games-table. The walls were covered with framed photographs.

The journalist blinked rapidly, in the bright light. McGuire was waiting with a soft drink in his hand. He rarely drank during business hours.

The American greeted him with an open grin. 'Black Label, isn't it?' He missed nothing that went on in his place. 'Help yourself.'

He was a tall man with fine bones. Good humour twinkled in the grey eyes. The fair hair would never lose its Californian bleaching. Only his well-cared-for hands betrayed his occupation.

'You were asking for me at the bar. What can I do for you?'

Kennedy, eyes veiled, hesitated. This was a hard, shrewd operator. He was in a tough racket, although now legal in Britain, still frowned upon by many. The laws concerning gambling were a bit vague and most operators found them-selves perched on the fence. He was sure that the American was straight, but if not he could find himself in deep trouble.

'I'm sure that you will have read of that cop killing last night. Was Detective Inspector Houston in here earlier in the evening?' McGuire was not the type of man to play clever games with. Better to give it to him direct.

Shutters dropped over the smiling grey eyes. 'Do you have anything to suggest he was?'

Kennedy tossed the book of matches over. 'Found in his pocket.'

'Yeah, that's one of ours.' There was no uneasiness in the tone. 'But he could have picked it up any time.'

The shutters flicked open for a moment and Kennedy thought he spotted a flash of worry. He sighed and shook his head gently.

'On a copper's salary Houston could not have afforded toothpicks in this place!'

The gambler smiled thinly. 'Christ! He was here sometime mid-evening.'

Lazily McGuire dropped into one of the armchairs. Reaching inside his dinner jacket he withdrew a thick bundle of notes. 'He talked about this — money.'

More specifically, hot money. With the big spate of robberies he reckoned there must be a lot of hot money about to be disposed of. And one of the best places to do this is a casino. Racecourses were also good.

Had McGuire heard of anyone spreading out unusually large amounts?

'I was not able to help him. I am an American. If I was caught stepping out of line I would be out of the United Kingdom on the first plane. So I make sure this place is as clean as a whistle. But I promised I would ask around the other operators in the city. And that's the truth.'

There was a knock and the heavy entered. The cashier wanted to see the boss. Some query about a cheque.

McGuire excused himself. 'Help yourself to another drink. I will be right back.'

He wandered aimlessly about the room. Most of the photographs confirmed that the gambler was also a keen sportsman. They showed him with fishing-rods, guns and horses. Some were obviously taken back in the States. Others were unmistakingly Scotland. McGuire holding up a 20 lb salmon. Crumpled stags at his feet. The river and mountain backgrounds were familiar.

His gaze fastened on a spot above the writing-desk. A lighter square on the wall showed that another photograph had hung there, but it had been taken down. It was amongst the Scottish selection.

On impulse he tried the desk drawers. One was locked. He had his hand in his pocket for his knife when the door swung open. He turned nonchalantly to find McGuire returning.

'I was admiring your photographs. I did not know you were into the open-air scene.'

'I get away as much as possible — and that is not half enough. I guess I'm just a country boy at heart.'

The reporter remarked casually about the missing photograph.

'Oh, that one!' replied McGuire hurriedly. 'It fell off the wall the other day and smashed. Must get it repaired.'

Kennedy found a quiet corner at the end of the bar. The place had filled up, but the buzzing conversation went over his head unnoticed. The casino boss had lied in his teeth. When alone he had admired the highly polished surface of the writing-desk. A deep shine without a blemish. A heavy photograph frame falling at least four feet would have marked it badly.

That photograph had been taken down deliberately. His instincts said it was important. He had to see it.

The head waiter found him a table and he treated himself to a well-done steak and bottle of good red wine. He attacked the meal with enthusiasm. He allowed himself to relax and enjoy the food. It was not until the coffee and brandy stage that he set his wits to the task of getting a glimpse of that photograph. He was certain it was in that locked desk drawer. Slowly a plan formulated in his mind and a smile twitched his lips.

It was nearly midnight when he returned to the gaming-room. He bought some chips and merged into the background. He wandered from table to table, winning a little, losing a little.

In the early hours the punters began to

thin out. It was time to make his first move. From a particularly dark spot he watched the entrance to the ladies' cloakroom. After about twenty minutes of observing the comings and goings, he was sure that it was empty — for a couple of minutes at least.

Sauntering over to the door, he swiftly sidestepped in. For a second he hovered awaiting exclamations of shock and surprise, ready with his embarrassed apologies. But it was deserted.

Small dressing-tables with large mirrors lined the wall. They were littered with the crumpled debris of what makes up ammunition in the sex war. The sickly scent of a thousand perfumes hung heavy like gunsmoke.

Five steps took him into the toilets. A dozen cubicles stretched down one side. He locked himself in the last one.

The final girl had left about an hour ago but he stayed put. There would be a security man who would check the premises after the club closed.

Thirty minutes crawled by before the powder-room door opened and a deep voice cried out, 'Anyone in there?' The door closed. Kennedy smiled in satisfaction. Even when the club was closed the security officer would not go into the ladies' loo. No Britisher would. It just was not done.

He let another hour pass before making his way to McGuire's private room. He pulled aside the heavy curtains to let in the glow of the streetlights. It was enough. A minute's work with the penknife and the drawer slid smoothly open. A framed photograph lay there . . . and it was not smashed. He carried it over to the window.

A rowing-boat was drawn up on a stony beach. The gambler was leaning against it holding a fishing-rod. In the background, an imposing castle clung to a high rock. The journalist felt a swift pang of disappointment. The photograph told him nothing.

Yet McGuire had thought it important enough to take down and hide away.

He replaced it in the drawer. Now to get out of there.

Standing behind a drape at the top of

the Adams staircase he could see the middle-aged security man drowsing at the reception desk below. A red light began to flash on a board at his shoulder and a bell tinkled. The man jerked awake and snatched up the phone.

'Fire Service, please. Club Scarlet here. Our alarm system shows a fire in the ladies' cloakroom. Yes I will do that.'

He rushed over and unlocked the front doors. Then grabbed a fire-extinguisher and raced up the stairs.

The fire-appliances roared past Kennedy as he walked to his car. All they would find would be a smouldering wastepaper-basket. Some careless bitch must have dropped a lighted cigarette into it. That's what they would think. He grinned to himself.

The cuttings library of his newspaper was the graveyard of a million stories. Every day each story was cut out and carefully filed away in its proper place. Photographs were painstakingly catalogued. Reference books lined the walls. No matter what the subject was, the librarian would dig out some information on it.

He requested all the photographs on file of Scottish castles. There were hundreds. Leafing through them, he cast them aside one by one. Then there it was — a tall square keep in cold grey granite seemingly an integral part of the rock it perched upon. Castle Inverawe on the Island of Bargrennan.

The island on which George Campbell had died. The island Alex Houston had visited just before he died. And the island that McGuire did not want to be associated with.

The long table in the library was covered with cuttings, books, maps and photographs. He had learned a lot about Bargrennan in the last hour. It was an island in the Parish of the Small Isles. Oval in shape, it was ten miles long by seven at its broadest point. Its western shores were battered by the Atlantic and a graveyard for shipping. Its surface was mainly an irregular mass of mountainous heights. The east side facing the mainland was indented by a narrow loch about two miles long. It was around this loch that most of the population lived and worked.

The small port of Inverawe was on the south side of the loch. And opposite the town, Inverawe Castle crowned a high rocky peninsula. The population was just over 600 souls.

The island's history was the usual bloody one to be found in Scotland. The castle had been built in the late 1200s by Angus McRee. One of the few Highlanders to support Robert the Bruce, he had been one of that warrior king's hatchet men in the fight against the English.

But in the rebellion of 1745 the McRee's backed the wrong side. This resulted in the douce folk of Edinburgh being entertained to some bonnie hangings. McRees being the main participants.

The island slipped into obscurity for the next 200 years. Except for a brief revival during World War II when a Coastal Command airstrip was built near the castle nothing happened to disturb the peace of the island's calm.

Then five years ago the Chief of the Clan McRee died. An old bachelor with few close relatives. The title went to the grandson of a far-off cousin who had emigrated to America at the turn of the century.

A few weeks after the old man was put to rest the new Chief arrived. Roderick McRee was rich, even by American standards. He was so taken with the island that he wrapped up his interests in America and settled in the castle.

For hundreds of years Bargrennan had been an economic desert. It had barely survived on a little poor farming and some fishing. Its one export — people.

Roderick McRee changed all that with New World enthusiasm. He used his capital to revitalize the island. He poured money into the farms and bought new fishing-boats. But more important he attracted people back.

He encouraged youth organizations to use the island for their activities. He opened a leadership school in an old tower and industries throughout the country sent their bright young executives there for leadership training.

He breathed new life into an island forgotten by time and dying of neglect.

There was a photograph of the Chief.

He was dressed casually in the kilt and open-necked shirt. His sleeves were rolled up showing muscular arms. Despite being in his early fifties, there were few streaks of silver in the thick brown hair. A strong beak of a nose hooked out of a hawklike face. Proud eyes and thin mouth showed he was self-sufficiently aggressive. Not a man to take liberties with easily.

Bargrennan linked Campbell, Houston and McGuire. But did it really mean anything? Was there menace in the tenuous connection.

He met Margaret for lunch in a small restaurant overlooking the river. She was cool and serene in a light summer dress. A cashmere cardigan was thrown over her shoulders. The lines of despair had gone but her eyes still mourned. She sipped at a gin and tonic.

'You mentioned on the phone a link between this fellow McGuire and Alex,' she said tonelessly. 'Something to do with an island.'

While they ate — she only picked at her food — he related his investigations. He managed to make her smile as he described how he had set fire to the club in order to escape unnoticed.

'There was no real risk of sending the place up. If the alarm had not gone off it would have burned itself out in the bucket.'

The meal was a failure. The dead detective was a spectre between them.

They strolled along by the river. The warm sun did little to melt their reserve towards each other. The girl stopped and leaned over the parapet watching the slowly moving water. Odd bits of rubbish bounced along with the current.

She agreed that the Bargrennan thing was worthwhile following up.

'But I am going away tomorrow for a few days,' she added stoically. Her cheeks were as white as graveyard marble. 'I do not know where. I am just going to drive and drive. I must get away from everything that reminds me of Alex for a while. Even you, David.

'Is that wrong of me?'

There was an appeal for understanding in her voice that he could not ignore.

'I think it is an excellent idea. Let the

memories fade a little. Come on, I will walk you back to your office.'

There did not seem anything else to say.

The MG was in a nearby car park. Small and neat, it made its modern neighbours seem drab. He let his gaze run proudly over it before climbing into the bucket seat.

He was just about to start up when his eyes locked on the bonnet. His hand froze. The sun was suddenly terribly cold. His vision blurred for a moment, then cleared.

Gingerly he eased out of the small car. Inch by inch — it must not rock. Two sets of oily fingerprints marred the otherwise gleaming bonnet. They were not his. He turned his head quickly. Maybe one of the other drivers using the car park had had a look at the old model. But they would have been businessmen or shoppers — and would not have oily hands!

Cautiously he raised the bonnet a fraction. Searching fingers found nothing. He opened it fully. Five sticks of explosive were strapped to the engine and wired to the starting system.

Someone was really desperate to get him out of the way permanently. He thought briefly of getting in touch with Macdonald, but cast the idea aside. He doubted if those oily fingerprints were on file either. It would worry his enemy more if he did nothing.

He was scared stiff but felt very, very alive. It was like being back in the jungle or in the Aden wilderness. Every minute might be the last and had to be savoured.

He dismantled the bomb and hid it behind the seat. He might just get a chance to return it to its rightful owner one day.

Driving across town, he kept an eye on his rearview-mirror, but no-one was following. If he wanted to live he had better start hitting back.

George Campbell had lived in a tall red sandstone building. Grim and solid, it overlooked a public park. The dead policeman had lived on the top flat. He knocked on the door opposite. The brass nameplate read 'Currie'.

A thin, severe, middle-aged woman opened it.

'Mrs Currie?'

'Miss,' she corrected harshly.

She could only have been a spinster, thought Kennedy. He apologized and said he was making inquiries into her neighbour's accident. He expected the door to slam, but her dull eyes brightened and the slash of a mouth managed what might have been a smile. She asked him in.

The flat was neat and clean with everything in its place. Over-furnished with old but well-cared-for pieces.

'George died some time ago. Why are you so interested in the accident now, Mr Kennedy?' Her voice was surprisingly soft and he noticed the use of Campbell's Christian name.

He showed her his press card. 'Anything you can tell me about Sergeant Campbell might help me in some other inquiries I am making. I can assure you it is very important.'

His brief explanation must have convinced her because she opened right up about George Campbell and her friendship with him.

The policeman had been her only real close friend. Two lonely people, living closely to each other, but still valuing their independence and freedom. Too old to change.

Once a week, on a Sunday evening, he had crossed over for dinner. 'We would always sit and talk after the meal,' said the woman sorrowfully.

He asked about Bargrennan. She confirmed that he went up there often. He had kept on the family cottage just outside Inverawe. He always flew up.

'A terrible waste of money,' she commented with a spinster's thriftiness. 'Train and boat would have been cheaper.'

Kennedy watched her closely as he asked, 'Did he tell you anything out of the ordinary before his last trip?'

A tense, thoughtful expression passed over her prim features. No, but when he had returned from his previous trip — that had been in the spring — she could see something was wrong.

'In what way?'

Usually he was full of the holiday when

70

he got back. This time he had little to say. And the following day he had written to a firm of private investigators in America.

Kennedy jerked with surprise. 'And how did you find that out, Miss Currie?'

'Because I posted all his letters. I remember thinking it was funny at the time. I thought real policemen did not think much of those sort of people. He told me he was trying to trace some relatives over there.'

'Did Sergeant Campbell have any other friends?'

Miss Currie shook her head slowly. He was a quiet man, not one for gallivanting. 'But wait a moment! He had one friend who used to visit about twice a year. His name was Captain Robertson and he is in the Merchant Navy. They served together during the war.'

She let a deep sigh escape her lips. 'George went right through the war safely. Then dies in a stupid accident within sight of his birthplace. Sometimes I find it hard to understand the ways of the Lord.'

At the door the thin spinster touched

his arm. 'Mr Kennedy, I am not a stupid old woman. You have not told me everything. No, don't deny it. Just be careful. When George left on that trip he was frightened, very frightened.

'When it is all over come and have tea with me.'

As Kennedy ran down the stairs he realized he would do just that.

5

'I am not happy about this, not happy at all,' frowned Sir Colin. 'Someone tried to blow you to smithereens. The police must be informed.'

'And what can they do to protect me? Put a guard on my home and have another following me around? That wouldn't stop this killer. They would just get it as well.

'I think I am on to something and that is why they are trying to get rid of me. I want to stay loose and free — even for just a few more days.'

He had briefed the newspaper's owner on his progress. Sir Colin agreed that although slim the Bargrennan line was promising. But there was something Kennedy still wanted to check out.

A couple of phone calls to shipping companies had produced a Captain William Robertson with the Clyde and Far East Trading Company. His ship, the

SS Diamond, was at present in Singapore.

A call had been put through to the paper's correspondent in that city. He had been instructed to find Robertson and get him to a phone.

'What do you expect to learn from this man?' asked Sir Colin.

'I don't know,' grimmaced his reporter. 'But other than Miss Currie, he seems to have been Campbell's only friend.'

But he had a feeling that it was vital to talk to the seaman. Someone had said something that niggled at the back of his mind. Robertson might be able to turn that niggle into hard fact.

The phone jerked him out of his revery. It was Singapore. The sailor's gruff voice was clear despite the distance and his puzzlement was clear in his tone.

'Captain, are you friendly with a Glasgow police officer, George Campbell?' asked Kennedy at once.

Robertson replied they had served together during the war and were still good friends. He visited him on every trip to Glasgow.

'I am sorry, but I have some bad news,' said Kennedy carefully. He explained the full facts of the sergeant's death.

Sir Colin watched him closely as he listened to the seaman's reaction to the details. The angular face hardened and the green eyes gleamed over the receiver. Barely suppressed excitement flowed from him.

Robertson went on for some length, his voice only a vague mumble to Sir Colin. Finally Kennedy thanked him, promised to keep in touch and hung up.

'Well, what did he say, man?'

'Captain Robertson has just proved that Campbell was murdered!'

The two men had served together on an armed merchant cruiser during the war. It had been sunk in the South Atlantic by a German pocket battleship. They had spent twenty days drifting on a raft before being picked up by a patrolling destroyer.

'It is because of that experience I know that George was murdered,' Captain Robertson had explained over the phone. 'We spent months in hospital and George never went back to sea again. He just could not step aboard a ship again. If he tried he was physically ill — even if it was lying alongside. That is why he always flew to Bargrennan.

'When he went out in that boat, he was either unconscious or already dead. George Campbell could not have died in a boating accident. He was murdered!'

★　★　★

The sun was just a faint red line across the eastern horizon when he gunned the MG out of the garage. He had a long way to go and wanted out of the city before daylight.

His boss had reluctantly agreed that he go to Bargrennan. 'I doubt if Robertson's claim would be enough for the police to reopen their inquiries. But I accept that Campbell could have been murdered up there. And Houston killed because he suspected the truth. Maybe he had even dug up something. But it is the reason for the killings that is still baffling. I am an islander myself and murder is rare on them.'

Kennedy agreed. He doubted if anyone had died violently on Bargrennan since the last clan raid three hundred years previously.

Sir Colin had also been for informing the police of his plans, but the reporter had begged for forty-eight hours. 'I have no facts to support my story. Give me that to find some.'

As he cruised along the empty streets he kept glancing in his mirrors. And was not really surprised to find a car on his tail. There were two men in it.

Over the last couple of days his sense of danger had become much more acute. Finely tuned nerves twanged away like fiddle strings. The touch of fear that tickled the back of his skull did not bother him. Fear kept things in perspective. He just had to keep it from turning into blind panic.

Normally he would have waited and not jumped in with both feet. But soon his route would lead him out into the country. That car was a large, powerful foreign job and could outrun the MG on the straight. If he was going to shake them it had to be now.

He turned left. It followed. Another unheralded turn and it stayed with him. No doubt about it now. The MG was nippy with first-class acceleration and could turn on a sixpence. He must not give them the opportunity to use their speed.

Slamming his foot down, he felt the kick at the base of his spine as the car leapt forward. He swung across the front of an early-morning bus. The horn blasted in his ear.

Tyres shrieking, he kept the little vehicle turning and swerving. The larger car would not be shaken off. A thin evil smile twisted his face. He was not being chased but was leading his pursuers on a route of his own choosing.

The big car was gaining slightly but he could not let it get too close. Digging into his stomach was the comfortable bulge of a Colt 45 pistol. His only souvenir of the jungle war. It felt good.

The long searching headlights picked out what he had been looking for. He swept up past a school. There it was

. . . the opening to a narrow lane.

He heaved on the steering-wheel and went into a swaying turn. For a heart-stopping moment, it seemed as if the MG was going over, but with a bounce it shot into the lane like a bullet.

The shrieking of tortured rubber followed him as the hunters hung on to his tail. The lane ran down the side of the school playing-fields. On that side was a high steel link fence to prevent the kids from escaping. On the other, the wall of an empty warehouse.

The steering-wheel shook violently as the MG thudded over broken Victorian cobbles. He was trapped in the centre of huge blazing headlights only feet behind. His engine roared in protest as it reached its limit.

The two cars hurtled towards the end of the lane. Kennedy's eyes stared fixedly down the long tunnel of white light. And suddenly there they were — sticking up out of the cobbles — two black iron stanchions!

He aimed the MG at the space between them. It was a small car, but was it small enough? The opening seemed to get narrower and narrower as he approached it. It took all his willpower to keep his foot flat on the pedal. A scream started to work up from his lungs. A scream he could not stop.

Then he was through! He had not time to feel relief. An explosion swept the sports car before it. A blast of heat swamped him. He had to fight desperately to keep the car on four wheels. He managed to brake in a patch of shadow.

The other vehicle was a ball of fire. The red glare was reflected off the low clouds. Travelling at 80 miles an hour it had come to an instant halt against the stanchions. Designed to keep Victorian carts out of the lane they were also extremely effective in stopping £7,000 worth of 20th-century machinery.

His way took him north up Loch Lomond. Down at the south end of the magnificent stretch of water the hills were softly swelling with a green pastoral appearance. Prosperous farms could be seen on the hill slopes. Black dots of cattle weaved over the hills on their way to the morning milking.

Gradually the loch narrowed and the mountainous Highlands took over. Fierce purple peaks threatened to fall and crush him. Their bare, jagged ridges presented a bold and broken outline against the clearing morning sky.

He felt superb. Nothing could just beat the thrill of escaping death. He felt no shame for killing those two men. They had been hunters. But the prey had hit back.

Leaving the blue waters behind, he climbed up over the bleak moors and hills. The clachans of Crianlarich, Tyndrum and Bridge of Orchy were soon behind his spinning wheels. The MG raced across Rannoch Moor and plunged into the gloom of Glencoe.

Each mountain above him was blessed with a Gaelic name. Ugly in print, but beautiful when spoken.

The Bargrennan Ferry was situated past Fort William and well into Morar. Two cottages and a concrete strip showed him he had reached the terminal. The ferry was a converted landing-craft. Old, but ideal for the task.

The ramp lay flat on the concrete. The tank deck gaped open to gulp the MG into itself. He backed into the craft where a sailor assisted him to get into position.

The skipper was hanging over the wing of the bridge when Kennedy went up on deck. Young and tough-looking, the heavy white sweater emphasized the deepness of his chest. He had a seaman's searching blue eyes.

He smiled down in a friendly manner.

Kennedy grinned back. He slapped a rail. 'I wonder if the old girl saw any action?'

'I don't know about that but she has been through a few hairy crossings here. Navy yourself?'

'No, but I have a cousin who was a chief petty officer. He served in one of these in the Far East.'

'Lousy sea boats if you have a weak stomach. But it should be a good crossing today, sir.'

'I sincerely hope so. When do we sail?'

'In a few minutes when the school bus arrives.'

The skipper caught the question in Kennedy's eyes. 'There is no senior secondary school at Inverawe. The older children have to go over to the mainland. Before the Chief opened this service they had to board there and only get home on holidays.'

He spoke with enthusiasm of McRee's generosity. He also owned and operated the plane that linked the island with BEA flights at Inverness. It used the old wartime airstrip. There was a touch of an accent in his tone that the reporter could not recognize. But he was not a Highlander that was for sure.

A single-decked bus swept round the bend and laughing teenagers rushed up the ramp. The skipper vanished into the wheelhouse.

Kennedy leaned on the rail to take in the view. The sun reflected off the water like a million diamonds. Faint shadows on the horizon were islands or approaching clouds.

Salt spray flew over the blunt bows as the craft smashed across the few miles to Bargrennan. The air was so clear that he could see whitewashed cottages clinging to the shore. He could spot the smoke of Inverawe well up the loch, but the castle was hidden below a low ridge.

He pulled out an Ordnance Survey map to study it again. It was always good to know the land you may have to fight over. And if he was right, he might be in for a bit of a tussle over there.

At any rate, he would not be doing much driving. One road curved round from the township to pass the castle and peter out at the airstrip. Another followed the south side of the loch for a couple of miles before it also came to a dead end. And the last one circled round the fertile basin surrounding Inverawe to serve the farms.

Once in the loch, the water was calmer. The hills formed a bastion from the wind. Now he could see the castle on its high rock. The silver granite shone bravely in the sun. The Chief's own banner fluttered from a flagpole on the highest turret. McRee was at home.

Inverawe's stubby pier had a few fishing-boats alongside. Behind the town, the rounded tip of Cairn Hill was prominent.

Turning quickly, he caught the skipper's gaze on him. He was not smiling now. Kennedy had seen that look before . . . over the sights of a rifle!

6

Kennedy held up a corner of the bar in the Inverawe Hotel. He had just finished a plain but satisfying meal. The fish had been so fresh that he could still taste the sea salt on it. Now he nursed a whisky and listened. It was surprising what a man could learn by shutting up and keeping his ears open.

The hotel was about the largest building in town. Solidly built, it faced the pier.

He had been met at the reception desk by an extremely attractive girl. A fraction over five feet, she was trim in every way. Very short black hair and a tiny nose made her face impish. Prominent cheekbones and firm chin showed courage and determination.

He introduced himself and found to his surprise that she was the owner of the place — Mrs Isla Armstrong.

As he signed the register he deliberately

revealed his cover story. He had come up to gather information to write an article on the island and its revival. If Inverawe was like any other small community, the whole island would know about him within the hour.

'Your room is at the top of the stairs,' she said. 'If you leave your luggage here, John the barman will take it up. And if you feel like a bath after your trip I would advise you to get in quickly. There is a group of young archaeologists staying here at the moment. They are working on some prehistoric burial grounds on the island. They are due back soon and hog all the hot water.'

He pushed the glass forward for a refill. The barman was a short, stocky man of about sixty with tiny blue scars on his face and hands that spoke of earlier years down the pits.

He obviously thought a lot of his boss. 'She is a fine lassie.' There was a hint of warning in his voice.

'What is her husband like?'

'He's deid!'

It took another whisky and one for

himself to get the little man to elaborate. Alistair Armstrong had been a civil engineer from Edinburgh. He had come up to work for McRee and lived in the hotel. The girl was already running it on her own then. Her father and mother had passed on while she was in her late teens.

'A good lad. The lassie was fair taken wi' him and in nae time they were married. The accident happened about nine months later. Alistair was a great boy for walking the hills. One night he went out for a stroll and never came back. In the morning we found him deid at the foot o' some cliffs on Cairn Hill. He must have slipped.'

He wandered out to have a look at the town before it got dark. Inverawe's principal buildings faced the loch — the hotel, main shops, bank, council offices and police station. There was one constable responsible for the whole island. He lived behind the station.

A few narrow streets curled up from the water's edge. Here were more shops, coal yard, post office and primary school. The local tradesmen and fishermen lived in low cottages right at the back of the township. The only church, with the manse alongside, was on a small knoll at the top of the town.

Up a cobbled lane he came across another pub — the Saracen's Head. Easing his way through hard-drinking fishermen and farmers he bought a pint. For the price of a black rum he got some more information from a retired skipper seated at the fire.

The old man spoke of a new jeep track the Chief had built right round the island. Another snippet proved more interesting. The new young people who had come to work on Bargrennan were well liked by the locals. They had integrated well with the community. But McRee's own staff kept aloof. They worked, ate and slept at the castle or at the tower at the south end of the island. They rarely came to the dances or other social functions.

The hotel bar was almost empty when he returned. John pushed over a nightcap.

'Are you staying here as well?' The question was drawled in a clear American accent.

He turned to face the newcomer. About forty, the man had the build of an out-of-training heavyweight. He had chubby features and long silver hair. The round face was burned Apache brown.

'Aye. I should be here for a few days, maybe a week.'

The American introduced himself as Richard Carson. He was clearly lonely and wanted to talk. He was a marine engineer and ran a firm that specialized in engines for yachts, fishing-boats and other small craft. Over in England on business he had read of Roderick McRee and his island. The Chief was examining the possibility of starting a boat building yard. Carson was trying to get in on the ground level and supply engines for the project.

Kennedy realized it was after closing time but that the barman made no move to close up. He seemed to be waiting for someone and kept glancing at the door. He smiled when finally a very tall, gangling man slid in.

The reporter took in the heavy black boots, dark trousers, blue shirt and black tie. The policeman's uniform jacket had been discarded for a thick tweed jacket.

'Sorry I am late, John. There was a wee bit of a tulsie at the Saracen's Head that required my attention. A dram, please.'

Carson slapped the newcomer on the shoulder. 'Have this one on me and meet our latest arrival, David Kennedy. Constable Jock McKay keeps the peace in these parts.'

Watery eyes smiled briefly. 'Mrs Armstrong mentioned to me earlier that you were staying here. I take your newspaper and have read your stuff. But are you not a crime reporter, Mr Kennedy? You will not find much of that in Inverawe.'

'That's right, Jock. But I needed a break and overheard the features editor talking about getting one of his chaps to do a piece on this place. I volunteered. So you really could call it a working holiday.'

The American yawned. 'I'm bushed. So if you will excuse me I am off to get my head down. Goodnight, gentlemen.'

Kennedy went to follow but a gaunt hand rested on his forearm.

'I would like a talk with you,' said the

policeman quietly. 'Come round to my place tomorrow evening after dinner and have a dram. I might be able to help you write that story.' There was real bitterness in his tone.

He had just finished breakfast when the attractive hotel-owner told him he was wanted on the phone. The voice at the other end was high-pitched and tremulous. He was not sure whether it was a man or woman.

'Good-morning, Mr Kennedy. My name is Brown and I am the Chief's secretary. Would it be convenient for you to come over to the castle about 11.00? The Chief would like to meet you and offer you lunch.'

As he drove up to the castle, he realized it was much larger than he originally thought. The main keep was perched right at the end of the rocky peninsula. Its seaward walls blending into the living stone that plunged down into the deep waters of the loch.

It was a formidable fortress. The keep was five storeys high and a curtain wall followed the outline of the peninsula. At each corner it was strengthened by semicircular buttresses. In the centre of the wall on the landward side was a main gateway that passed under a protecting tower.

The area within the walls was laid out into an attractive garden with shrubs and fruit trees. Against the wall next to the keep were the old stables. He guessed used as garages now. Just to the west of the castle was a small harbour. Berthed there was a large ocean-going motor cruiser.

A tough-looking gatekeeper stopped the car as it swung between the strong iron gates. 'Good-morning, sir. You will be Mr Kennedy. The Chief is expecting you.'

A polite smile cracked the bull-like features and sharp eyes roved over the MG. Placing a hand on the low windscreen, he examined the interior closely.

'Sorry if I seem rude, sir. But I have not come across one of these little beauts in years. You have put a lot of work in her.'

'Thanks. If you would like a closer look, come down to the hotel.'

He drove slowly round the shingle drive aware that he and the car had just been given a very polite but efficient once-over.

The main entrance was on the first floor. In the old days there would have been a slender wooden staircase up to it that could have been removed quickly in the case of sudden attack. Now there were sweeping broad stone stairs.

The secretary was waiting for him — a severe, scrawny individual in a purple velvet suit. And a bloke — he thought. He nodded for Kennedy to follow him.

The main hall was immense and the highly polished floor would have been appreciated by an Olympic skater. Brown lead him up a twisted staircase to the Chief's Hall. It was smaller but still very impressive. Rudely pointed walls reached up to a wonderful vaulted ceiling. Sheep and deer skins stood in for rugs. Heavy wooden tables and chairs were grouped together before a huge fireplace.

Finally he was shown into a small comfortable room on the fourth floor.

The harsh granite was concealed behind rich panelling and expensive drapes. The furniture was a pleasant mixture of old and new. Definitely a lived-in room and not an ancient monument. This would be part of the castle that visitors rarely saw.

There was only time for a quick glance round when Roderick McRee stormed in — in a flurry of tartan and bronzed thighs. His eyes flashed as he smashed a fist down on a corner desk scattering papers and documents.

'Those bloody civil servants! They claim it is the unions that are bringing this country to its knees. They are damned wrong. It is those bastards in the Civil Service!'

He threw back his head and cursed those public servants with the best of obscenities from both sides of the Atlantic. The reporter listened with something akin to awe. It was a performance that would have abashed a chief petty officer stoker.

Suddenly he stopped in mid-flow and broke into loud laughter and stepped forward to grip his visitor's hand. 'My sincere apologies. But I have been trying to get some information out of the Scottish Office in Edinburgh. I should have known better. I am not normally a cursing man but there are times . . . '

The Chief splashed whisky into a couple of glasses. He took a deep swallow of the fiery spirit.

'I need that. You deserve an explanation of my behaviour. A Royal Navy frigate appeared off the coast of the island this morning. I got on to the Ministry of Defence to find out what they are up to. Just being nosey. They had the bloody cheek to tell me that information was classified! I told them this was my bloody island and what they could do with their security.'

Finally the Scottish Office had admitted that the Navy was thinking of using the channel between the island and the mainland as a torpedo range.

'Over my dead body they will!' His anger was now naked and real.

This was not the sort of project he wanted on Bargrennan, he explained. A base would be built but it would not supply many local jobs. Roads would be constructed and scar the landscape. Hideous boxes of houses for the staff and their families. Then one day they would up and leave — but the scars would remain.

'What we are doing is natural and all our own work. We are using the island's own resources. Our own efforts for our own future. No outsiders will make use of us or our land.'

The outburst seemed to quieten the big man. He collapsed into a fireside chair with a swish of the dark green hunting tartan kilt and stretched out powerful legs.

'I can well understand your feelings,' declared Kennedy and then smiled. 'Like everyone else here you will already know I am on Bargrennan to write an article on the developments here. Your comments on the proposed range — minus the cursing, of course — would make good copy. Mind if I use them?'

'Go ahead. Might frighten the bastards. And I will only be too happy to help in any way. But get one thing clear.

Everything that is happening here is due to the energy and hard work of the islanders. I only pointed them in the right direction.'

'First can you tell me a bit about your background and life in America.'

McRee said his grandfather had emigrated to America from the island in the late 1800s. He had made good in his adopted country and died rich when the Chief was still a boy.

'He instilled into me a love of Scotland and particularly this part of it,' said McRee.

McRee had settled in Las Vegas just after the war and increased the family fortune in that gambling-mad town.

Then he had received a letter from an Edinburgh lawyer. A far-off relative had died. He was now the Chief of the Clan McRee.

He fell to thinking. For a long time he had been dissatisfied with his life. Maybe this was the chance he had been waiting for. He wrote to the Scots lawyer and requested a complete report on the state of things on the island.

'I was shocked at how bad they were,' he said. 'And I know this will sound naive, but I decided to come over and accept my responsibilities as Chief — become father of the clan. As they considered themselves in the old times.

'So I wrapped up all my business interests. My lawyers and accountants had coronaries. They had been living off me for years. Bargrennan is my life now.'

Kennedy was impressed. A Scots Lowlander, he had a friendly contempt for his Highland brother. They were more easy-going than the dour Lowlanders. But this man had touched a spark in the latent energy of the islanders and blew it into a blazing flame.

Yet somewhere on Bargrennan there might be a killer. And that man could ruin everything McRee had achieved.

The Chief spoke enthusiastically of his ventures into farming and fishing. His boats went to fishing-grounds all round Britain. Sometimes as far afield as Iceland.

His Adventure Training School was very popular with big business and industry. A couple of weeks tramping and climbing in the mountains and the natural leaders came to the fore.

And he was also pleased with his efforts in attracting young people to come and settle. Nearly one hundred had answered his call. Tired of the rat race, they wanted to do something really worthwhile.

'I have about forty men on my immediate staff,' he went on. 'They work here at the castle, at the Training School, on my farms and on some of the boats.

'They are key men. Each one hand-picked and on call seven days a week.'

Roderick McRee had stood up. The military-style khaki shirt and strong, stern good looks reminded Kennedy of a senior officer in a fighting Highland regiment. Gun metal eyes gleamed with an almost physical power.

'But come and have lunch and meet some of them. Once a week we get together for a simple beer and bite in the Chief's Hall. There will also be some of the local businessmen.'

His staff were mostly in their twenties. They seemed a friendly crowd and were attacking the long food-laden tables with the healthy appetites that comes from hard work in the open air.

A muted cheer greeted McRee. He waved to them and got the newspaperman a beer. 'Help yourself to food and then mingle. Get to know them. I have to make my rounds of the locals.'

Heaping a plate with chicken and salad, he stood to the side and looked about him. He could imagine the same scene under the same roof in times past. Lean, wolf-like warriors celebrating a raid on the clan's enemies. But instead of the Gaelic, the accents here came from all over the world. He picked up English, Irish, American and Australian.

But they had all one thing in common. They had an aim and were fit and healthy. He recalled the lad he had killed in Glasgow. A twist of fate and he could have been amongst this lot and not cold meat in a police mortuary.

A giant of a man pushed towards him. 'The Chief asked me to look after you. I am Jamieson and run the Adventure Training School. I am one of the few real Highlanders in this lot.'

Between stuffing slices of rare beef into his mouth, Jamieson pointed out some of the others. One tough character, older than the rest, in washed-out blue jeans was De Bere, a South African. He was in charge of the fishing-boats and skippered the big cruiser.

Kennedy chatted to Galbraith, the local bank manager, and was introduced to the Reverend McLeod, the minister. He was a little man, aged before his time.

The lunch party began to break up and McRee walked his guest to his car. 'If you want to talk to me again just come over.'

The journalist paused at his MG. 'By the way, I did not have a chance to mention it before. But I knew George Campbell quite well. Tragic business.'

The Chief rubbed the back of his neck. 'Yes it was that. And I feel partly responsible.'

'Why?'

'On that last day he came round to talk about a job after he retired. As he left he asked to borrow one of my boats to go fishing. Hours later George was dead!'

7

Kennedy shivered in the hot sun as he swung the open car out of the castle. The gatekeeper waved unnoticed.

George Campbell had had a deep psychological fear of boats. He would not have asked McRee to borrow one. But why would the Chief say that? Could he be in some way involved in the sergeant's death? But that would be incredible. There had to be a rational explanation to the puzzle.

On the nearside a rocky shingle beach sloped down to where the retreating tide tugged at the stones. On his right small green fields bordered by stone walls chequered the hillside.

Suddenly the steering-wheel jerked angrily in his hands and he fought for control. The front offside tyre had blown. He halted and climbed out. Crouching down, he ran his fingers over the rubber. A bullet slammed into the tarmac next to his right foot and gravel stung his face. For a thousandth part of a second his brain went numb and then, slapping both hands on the wing, he vaulted over the bonnet.

Pressing himself against the metal, he gathered his wits. He raised his head and the wind of a bullet made him duck again. This time he heard the crack. The sniper was about 300 yards away and to the right. He was most probably staked out in a clump of pine trees on the ridge.

He turned his head desperately. There was no cover for 200 yards. He was well and truly pinned down.

He eased his head round the bumper. Another bullet whipped past his cheek. The sniper had only to move some yards to the right and he would be a sitting target. He began to straighten. A running man was not an easy target. One deep breath and he would start a race against a high-powered bullet.

'Hi, Davie boy. What's up?'

Kennedy nearly keeled over with shock. A few yards away Carson straightened up out of an unseen fold in the ground.

'I was out for a walk, sat down and dozed off in the sun. Something just woke me up.'

Kennedy got up very slowly — ready to drop. His muscles cracked with tension. The only sound was the sad lonely cry of a curlew.

'I have a flat,' he croaked.

'Come on and I will give you a hand to change it. Then bum a lift back into town.'

The island's only policeman was standing outside the hotel when he drew up. 'McKay, I think we should have that chat now.' He turned towards the police office.

The blue uniformed man swung round in front of him. 'No, Mr Kennedy. In here.' He led the reporter into the hotel's small office. Isla Armstrong was working at some papers. She shot a surprised glance at the pair.

'She is involved in all this. Isla, the meeting has been brought forward.'

Turning the key in the door lock, McKay walked over to stand beside the girl. He stared at the tops of his boots for a moment before speaking.

'What are you really doing here, Mr Kennedy?'

'I told you last night — to write a feature story.' The journalist wanted this dour man to open the batting.

Isla was leaning forward with an intense burning in her dark eyes.

McKay snorted. 'I may be a simple Highland policeman, but I am not foolish enough to believe that.

'A Glasgow policeman dies here in an accident — or what looks like an accident. A senior city detective comes up for the funeral and then spends days snooping around. Then he is murdered.

'Next a well-known crime reporter arrives on Bargrennan. It all seems too much of a coincidence for my liking. Now why are you here?'

The girl's eyes were riveted on the reporter. She had an air of desperate expectancy. Her hands were clenched into tiny fists.

He had to make a decision. He need not say anything. But if he did it would have to be all.

'Okay, I expect you have the right. It is your damned island anyway.'

He told them of the terrible events back in Glasgow. Of Captain Robertson and the photograph in the Club Scarlet.

'No McGuire has ever stayed here,' interrupted Isla. 'But he could have been a guest at the castle.'

Kennedy was silent for a moment. Could Bernie have known McRee back in the States?

He neglected to tell them of the attempts on his own life. McKay was a cop after all and an investigation into the most recent one would just muddy the water.

'Now before I go any further, what is your angle in all this?'

There was a trace of satisfaction in McKay's direct stare. 'The usual investigation was carried out into George's death. McRee told of his request to borrow the boat. De Bere and Jamieson alleged they had given him a hand to push it out. The South African found the upturned craft the following morning.

'But I wasn't happy. You see George

and I were old friends and went fishing often, but always on the river. He always found an excuse not to fish the loch. I never really thought anything about it until after his death.

'But the Procurator Fiscal demands hard facts, not hunches from old policemen.

'But your story now confirms my own feelings. He was murdered and the Chief was involved in some way!'

Kennedy could feel an excited tingle in his spine. He turned to the girl. 'And your angle — where do you come into all this?'

'My husband, Alistair.' Her body was stiff and rigid and her face a mask. 'I know he was murdered!'

Armstrong had been a first-class mountaineer. And like most skilled climbers, he was a cautious man in the hills.

'When we walked on Cairn Hill he would never let me go near the edge of the cliffs. The rock is as smooth as glass and often wet. I made fun of his caution.'

And yet he was supposed to have slipped and plunged to his death over those very cliffs.

Kennedy sighed heavily. Even good climbers were sometimes careless.

'But he also had a connection with McRee,' interrupted McKay. 'He worked for him on the modernization of the castle.'

'I cannot really believe that the Chief has something to do with all this,' murmured Isla Armstrong. 'He always has struck me as a fine man doing his best for the island.'

They talked for a few minutes more then broke up promising to meet the following day.

The soft smir of summer rain was drifting in from the sea after dinner. He drew in a couple of breaths of moist air and retreated to the bar. About a dozen men were drinking quietly. De Bere was in a corner with two other McRee men.

John placed a whisky in front of him and then leaned over the bar. 'Listen, Mr Kennedy. My beer-cellar is right under Mrs Armstrong's office.' He had overheard everything that had gone on earlier. 'I just wanted you tae ken I'm yer man if there's trouble.'

He nodded his thanks. What a place! Not only the walls had ears but the floors also.

'Watch those three bastards at the end.' It was the barman again. 'They have got it in for you. And that South African is a bad sod.'

He controlled an impulse to turn his head. A fierce expectation filled him. His fingers trembled, not with fear but excitement.

De Bere sidled up alongside him. Kennedy still did not turn. A long minute dragged past. The dark skinned man broke first.

'I want to talk to you.' Rum fumes were heavy on his breath and his eyes were red-rimmed and hard. The other two had not moved.

The blood pounded in Kennedy's skull. For days he had been running and dodging. He felt degraded being unable to hit back. He wanted to smash something — or someone.

'I'm listening.'

The coarse face pushed forward. 'I don't like reporters. Keep putting their big snouts into places where they are not wanted. Get off Bargrennan!'

'I am sorry you feel that way,' said Kennedy in a placating manner. 'The Chief seemed quite happy to grant me an interview.'

He imagined a touch of sudden fear or alarm flitted through the angry eyes, but then it was gone. He was aware of what the seaman was up to. He was tough and could fight, but something inside was lacking. He had to talk himself into a battle. But despite that, the South African was no coward and would take it as well as dish it out.

'He does not know pressmen like I do. You will go back to the mainland and write lies about us. British journalists are all the same. You come out to my country and then write lies about how we oppress the poor blacks. I bet you are even a nigger-lover.'

Spittle dribbled from the corners of his mouth. This was it! De Bere would explode into action at any moment. He had to knock the man off balance.

Kennedy looked round the bar nervously as if seeking support. The others turned away. They wanted no part of it. He was on his own. A sly grin split the sailor's face. This was going to be easy.

Then Kennedy leant forward and in a low voice that only De Bere could hear muttered: 'You could call me a nigger-lover. Just like your mother was when you were conceived.'

The implication of what the smiling Scot has just said staggered the man for a second. Then an uncontrollable fury burst in his brain. He let loose a wild swing with his right fist. Kennedy slapped it almost casually aside. The square chin was wide open. Everyone in the bar heard the thud of his fist connecting. De Bere's legs buckled at the knees. A straight left lifted him back against the bar and he hung there, shaken and dazed but not beaten.

With a roar, he snatched up a bottle and dived at his grinning opponent. Kennedy stretched inside the out-stretched arms and drove his knee hard into the unpro-tected crutch. With a nerve-tearing shriek, De Bere folded up. And his twisted face met a well polished brogue on the way down. He snapped back with a scream and swayed on his heels. The reporter placed a hand on the ruined face and pushed him back into the arms of his dumbfounded friends.

'Get this garbage out of here,' he ordered harshly. Hate filled their features as they dragged him groaning from the bar.

Uproar erupted and hands slapped his back. John handed him a clean towel to wipe the sweat from his face.

'And I was worried aboot ye, Mr Kennedy. You crucified the bugger!'

Kennedy woke to find Inverawe shrouded in a cloying white mist that whirled and weaved through the lanes and vennels of the old township. It was the Sabbath and the mist emphasized the stillness. Unseen seagulls gave out mournful cries like lost damned souls wandering in a white Hades. Until the weather changed, movement was practically impossible.

Mid-afternoon he was reading in the lounge when Isla Armstrong hurried in with worry clouding-her eyes and beads of moisture clinging to her shining black hair like tiny pearls.

She had just come from the manse. The minister was worried about Jock McKay. The policeman was an elder in the kirk and should have rung the bells that morning. But he did not turn up. Thinking him ill, the Reverend McLeod had gone down to the police office after lunch. It was locked up and there was no answer to his knocking. He tried neighbours and friends but no-one had seen McKay that day.

Kennedy attempted to calm the girl's fears. He was most probably up at one of the remote farms on something or other.

'No. I have a feeling that Jock is in trouble. Please help me find him.'

The entry to McKay's home was in a lane at the rear of the police office. He knocked and shouted. There was not even an answering echo from the mist. The curtains were still drawn on the windows.

'David, his Land-Rover is still in the garage. He might be lying ill inside.'

'Okay. When we do find him I hope he does not charge me with breaking and entering a police office.' His heavy shoe smashed against the lock.

The interior was cold and damp but the bed had been slept in. The blankets were thrown aside carelessly as if the man had risen in a hurry. The sitting-room fire was a bed of cold ash. Oatmeal was soaking in water in a pot on the cooker. McKay had not eaten breakfast.

His eyes fell on a phone in the hall. 'If he was called out suddenly, would the exchange know about it?'

'They might. It is still a manual exchange. We go automatic next year. I'll ask the operator.'

He was examining the sergeant's desk when an agitated Isla rejoined him. McKay had called the castle. She had got on to McRee and had just had a very disturbing conversation with him.

According to the Chief, McKay had contacted him very early that morning. He wanted to get over to the mainland in a hurry. It was urgent business. As the ferry did not run on a Sunday, could the Chief help?'

'As it was I was able to assist,' explained McRee. 'My cruiser was about to cast off to take an injured man across for hospital attention. He had been in a fight. Constable McKay joined it. The boat has excellent radar so the mist was no problem.'

The girl frowned at Kennedy. 'Urgent business? What could it have been?'

He shook his head. 'I can't see McKay leaving the island while there might be a killer on the loose. He would have got a relief here first. The telephone operators — who are they?'

She gave him a funny look. 'There are two of them and they work shifts. They used to work at the castle before working in the exchange.'

A horrible dread filled Kennedy. 'Jock never left Bargrennan. For my money he is either dead or being held in the castle.'

She braked a few hundred yards short of the castle and switched off the engine and lights. It was late evening but because of the mist it could have been the dead of night.

'Do you have to go, David?'

'Aye. Wait for an hour and if I have not returned get back home. If I have still not turned up in the morning find some excuse to go over to the mainland and phone Sir Colin Forbes from there. The island operators may be okay, but I do not want you taking any risks whatsoever.'

His rubber-soled shoes made no sound on the grass verge. Ahead a light bounced back off the white tentacles of mist — the gatehouse. The sturdy gatekeeper would not be straying far from his fireside tonight. The scent of woodsmoke was pleasant to his nostrils. He was about to slide up to the tall gates that lay invitingly open when he froze and sniffed quickly. There was another pungent smell in the air — cigar smoke!

An old woollen sock filled with sand felt comfortable in his hand. With the other he groped for a stone.

The guard was cold and miserable. Another hour before he could get a drink and something to eat. He took a last draw at the cigar before flicking the stub into the darkness.

What was that sound? It came from the other side of the road. There it was again. He edged nervously across the tarmac.

Nothing. It was the mist — right spooky. He would be jumping at his own shadow next.

He never noticed Kennedy slip through the gate behind him.

The newspaperman trotted across the short grass of the lawn. Every few yards he stopped to listen. The automatic stuck in his belt hurt his stomach.

He leaned against a slim apple tree and thought for a moment. If he was wrong, then he was going to feel damn foolish. Footsteps sounded high on his right. Someone was patrolling the curtain wall.

Under the protecting cover of the mist he swerved left. Where the wall met the castle a narrow stairway climbed up. He eased slowly out on to the walk. There seemed to be no-one on this side.

An iron-studded door opened on to a long narrow corridor cut through the thick castle walls. He crept along it. A mumble of voices grew louder. Suddenly his way was blocked by heavy drapes. He pushed them aside to see into the main hall.

The Chief of the Clan McRee was

standing stern and straight before the large fireplace. About a dozen of his staff were gathered about him. A tremor ran over Kennedy as he realized some of them were armed.

The tall man was obviously summing up a briefing. 'The journalist may be suspicious but that is all. If we keep our heads that is all he will have — suspicions. He needs hard facts. Make sure he does not get any.

'But make no mistake, he is a dangerous man. Efforts to dispose of him have ended in dismal failure. You all saw what happened to De Bere. The idiot tried to act on his own initiative and has paid for his foolishness.

'Kennedy will be dealt with in a few days when he returns to Glasgow — and before he reports to Sir Colin Forbes or the police. His death must not be linked with Bargrennan.'

McRee abruptly turned and left the hall and his men dispersed noisily.

Kennedy leaned wearily back against the cold wall. This was incredible. Sure he had had suspicions about the Chief. But inside he always believed there had to be a rational explanation of his statement about Campbell's wanting a boat. And that there was a perfectly reasonable solution to the mystery of McKay's disappearance.

But he never really had expected this. The man had an army in the castle and he had just heard his own sentence of death. And how did McRee know that he was reporting direct to Sir Colin?

He had no time to think of that now. Finding McKay — if he was alive — was his first priority.

Isla Armstrong had given him a good run-down on the castle layout. When her husband had been working on the modernization she had spent much time over here.

When the hall was cleared he ran to a far corner and pushed open a narrow door. Curved stairs led down to the kitchens and storerooms. He went to the right and at the end of the corridor was another door with a grill at face height. It was unlocked. Steps plunged down through living rock.

The chamber at the foot was in darkness. His searching fingers found a light-switch. It was a large square room with the old dungeons lining the walls. A charcoal brazier smoked in the centre. In one corner a low circular wall surrounded a well shaft.

But it was the still figure stretched out on a heavy wooden table that gripped his attention. He had found McKay!

The policeman was nearly naked and there was an ugly gun wound high on his chest. His face was a green-greyish colour and Kennedy thought he was too late. But the thin lips moved almost imperceptibly.

He got some water from a bucket and poured a little through the clenched teeth. Gently he bathed the twisted face and the deep eyes opened.

'Hold on, Jock. I'll get you out of here.'

McKay could only whisper. 'It's too late for me. I am bleeding inside and haven't got long. Listen.' There was a desperate urgency in his voice. 'I was daft. I decided to let my inspector on the mainland know what we suspected last night. But the operator claimed there was trouble with the line when we were cut off just after I got through.

'I know now he must have been listening. They came to my place and I was brought here. McRee tried to make me talk. Then this afternoon I was shot trying to escape.'

McKay's eyes closed wearily and he slipped away into unconsciousness.

A terrible rage filled Kennedy. But what was he going to do now? If he attempted to move the injured man, he would most probably kill him.

That next move was decided for him.

'Put up your hands and turn round slowly.'

8

The sub-machine-gun looked like a child's toy in the kilted guard's hands. A toy that could cut him in two. It pointed right at his middle and his stomach seemed to shrink as if in some way it could get further away from that threatening black hole.

The weapon jerked slightly. 'Get up those stairs.'

Kennedy did not move. 'No.'

The young guard blinked and his finger tightened on the trigger. 'Move . . . now!'

'No.'

McRee's man frowned. This was all wrong. He had the gun. The journalist should be scared stiff and jump when ordered. Anger and maybe a little fear made him shake. His finger tightened on the trigger.

Kennedy could feel the cold sweat running down his back. 'Remember McRee's orders. You can't kill me here.

Do that and the Chief will give you a one-way ticket to hell. That gun means damn all.' He forced a laugh.

The blood drained from the man's face. He had nearly made a terrible mistake. But what was he going to do?

He jumped as Kennedy spoke again. 'Relax, son. I will come with you in a moment. But first I am going over to the well and get some fresh water for my friend here. I would even give you a drink if you were dying.'

Relief surged through the guard. He had been taught how to handle a gun, but not situations like this.

Kennedy had to wipe the sweat from his hands before he could get a grip on the rope. His eyes flicked back and forth to the guard. Sooner or later he might make a mistake and he intended to be ready.

He was passing the glowing brazier when McKay let loose a piercing scream. For a split second, the lad's attention switched to the still figure.

The newspaperman's leg swung and the brazier tumbled. Red coals bounced over the stone floor and struck the bare legs under the kilt. The guard's yell was cut off as the heavy bucket crunched against the side of his skull.

'Thanks, Jock. I needed that edge.'

A faint smile fought through the pain. 'Get out of here, Kennedy. But first put that gun in my hand.'

Kennedy cocked the weapon and placed the limp fingers over the trigger-guard. 'The safety is off. Just press the tit. I don't know what the hell I am going to do, but I will try my best to get back with help.'

He made the curtain wall without incident. McRee was trying to keep intruders out — not in. The west wind had livened and the mist was thinning fast. A solitary star appeared. He had only minutes.

Isla greeted him with a relieved smile. 'I thought you . . . '

'Later,' he snapped. 'Back to the hotel and fast. The muck is about to hit the fan.'

John the little barman was in the office when they arrived. Quickly he related the happenings at the castle. The girl's face was ashen when he had finished, but also showed a stubbornness that he had not suspected.

'We must get help,' she urged. 'Maybe we can still save Jock.'

'I must get in touch with my boss. He is the very man to get action quickly.'

John coughed. 'You will not be able to get through to Glasgow by phone. The line is out of order. Mr Carson was trying to get in touch with London earlier, but the exchange claimed the underwater cable was damaged.'

'I wouldn't use the phone anyway, John. I'm sure the operators are in McRee's pocket. But I must get to the mainland. I'll go down to the pier and hire a fishing-boat to take me over.'

Pushing the girl aside, he ran for the pier. It was empty. The mist had gone and all the craft had sailed. The last boat to cast off was already a quarter of a mile out. Its navigation lights twinkled in the distance.

He was trapped.

The barman pointed across the loch. A

line of headlights was speeding along the road towards the town.

Kennedy thought furiously. The adrenalin that had pumped into his system during the castle adventure was still working away. His mind spun desperately seeking an idea.

'Hide in the hotel,' pleaded the girl.

No. That would be the first place they searched. Then he remembered his old infantry training — take the high ground. He was going to climb up into the mountains. It would take an army to find him in those craggy peaks. But he had to hurry. He only had minutes.

Back in his room he pulled on a pair of heavy boots and windproof anorak. Isla handed him a haversack with food, chocolate and a bottle of whisky. He tucked the pistol into his belt.

'Is there anyone in the hills who might help me?'

There were only two. Angus Kerr, a retired shepherd, lived on his own in a cottage on the west side of the island. And Mrs Grant, a widow — she had a cottage on the other coast.

At the door he remembered something.

He took a brown paper parcel from his case and pushed it into the haversack.

Isla handed him the key of the hotel's van. 'Better take it. That MG stands out a mile. Take care.'

She flushed as he touched her cheek with his fingers. When he had booked into her place she had thought him a nice ordinary chap. There was nothing about him that really impressed.

But was this the same man? The pleasant face seemed leaner and harder. The icy green eyes frightened her. And he handled that gun with easy familiarity.

The road petered out just below the ridge. There was no sign of pursuit as he clambered the last few yards to the top. The sky was a silver carpet of countless stars and despite the lack of moonlight, visibility was excellent.

A 'Mho in Teach Mhor — the Great Moss — stretched out before him. At night it was dark and threatening. A dangerous place of bottomless slime-covered bogs. And he had to cross it in the dark! By dawn it would be swarming with McRee's men. With his eyes on the blue cut-outs that were the mountains, he set out.

As the crow flies it was only about three miles, but he was no bird. Within minutes he was soaked from the knees down. Perspiration streaked his face as he ploughed through bogs and stepped high over dew-damp tussocks of rough grass.

Here and there the going was easier as he crossed patches of smooth grass cropped short by wandering sheep. Now and then he came across the tumbled walls of ancient summer shielings.

His spirits rose when he realized that he was climbing and stumbled onto a deer path. Quickening his pace, he circled huge boulders and curved round cliffs until he found himself standing on a ridge. Behind and below, he could pick out the lights of Inverawe like yellow stars.

His calf muscles ached with strain and his gaping mouth dragged in air. Cutting some heather with his knife, he placed it beneath an overhanging rock and eased his tired body down on the simple bed. It was the darkest part of the night and the silence was complete.

But sleep would not come. What the hell was going on and what was McRee up to? He was rich and respected. He was the saviour of Bargrennan. And yet the man was a killer. What was behind it all? And why did he need a private army?

God! He had wandered into something big. Too big for him by the looks of things. He was going to need all the skill and cunning drummed into him by foul-mouthed sergeants to come out of this lot with a whole skin.

Then he recalled that Alex Houston had said that he might have dug up a lead on those big bank raids. Could that be it? Was McRee tied up with them in some way?

No, that was ridiculous. The Chief was stuck up here in the Highlands and rarely left the island. The raids had taken place all over the United Kingdom — Glasgow, Aberdeen, Plymouth, Portsmouth, Liverpool, Newcastle, Hull and half a dozen other places.

He lit a cigarette and cupped the glowing end in his hand. In the far distance he could see the red and green navigation lights of some large ship on its way out into the Atlantic.

Suddenly it was as if a door in his mind had swung open. He had the answer! The clever bastard — no wonder the raiders always got away so easily.

He stubbed the cigarette out on a stone and burrowed into the heather again. This time he was asleep in seconds.

It was daylight when he opened his eyes. He lay still and catalogued the sounds about him. Birds whistling and wind rustling the bracken. Slowly he sat up. On a rock about twenty yards away perched a proud hawk. He smiled to himself. If his pursuers had been anywhere near, the bird would have been gliding along on the air currents high above.

Some stale bread and cheese washed down with a mouthful of whisky served for breakfast. Above him glens, corries and rushing burns slashed the purple and green slopes. It was among these walls, towers and peaks that he was going to find refuge.

The early-morning sun reflected on something bright on the far side of the moor. That would be McRee's men on his trail, but he still had about two hours' lead on them.

In the narrows between Bargrennan and the mainland the grey Navy frigate cruised on its business.

Spreading the Ordnance Survey map out on a flat rock he considered his next move. A day at the most was all he needed. Sir Colin had given him forty-eight hours and that was up. The tycoon would most probably try and phone first. And when he could not get through would get in touch with Chief Superintendent Macdonald. Then the detective would talk to his mates in the Highland Region. Then . . . Hell! It might take some time before help arrived from the mainland.

He could be at the bottom of a peat bog by then. And it would be McRee's word against that of Isla and John. And it did not take a genius to guess who would be believed.

It was at that moment he made a

132

decision. He was not going to run like a hare at the coursing waiting for the greyhound's jaws to crush its backbone. He was going to fight back.

He examined the map closely. He was on the lower slopes of Sgurr A'Ghreadaich — Peak of Torment. Before him was a small bowl containing a tiny lochan. On the other side the ground rose to a nick in the saddle between the Peak of Torment and Sgurr Na Stri — Peak of the Fight.

The men behind would not be the only ones out on the hills that day. Another lot would come up from the Adventure School at the southern tip. His finger rested on a spot on the west coast where the high sea cliffs were broken at one point by a narrow loch. At its head a glen pierced into the hills. Another obvious route for hunters. It was worth a look anyway.

Skirting boulders and rocky outcrops he made his way up through the nick. At the top was a plateau about two miles across and surrounded by mountain tops reaching for the blue heavens with broken, jagged fingers.

He started across the plateau that was the birthplace of half a dozen burns that tore towards the sea in different directions. Fortunately he found a deer pad that headed west.

At first he thought it was the buzzing of an angry bee. Then with a muttered curse he dived into some deep bracken. The insect that made that sound could have the sting of death.

The helicopter zoomed over the eastern ridge — a small two-seater job, ideal for its task. It swooped low over the plateau. From his hiding-place he watched it hover. The passenger was searching the immediate area with binoculars. There was a sudden roar as the pilot gunned the engine and it lifted away towards the north.

This was a serious problem. It meant keeping away from open ground and close to cover. It would slow him down and he would lose his precious mobility.

The ground was blessedly rough — deep beds of heather and bracken and tumbled rocks. A tiny stream twisted its way through the maze of shattered stone.

It was the beginning of the river that plunged into the glen that was his destination.

It rapidly increased in size until it was too broad to jump. A sudden roaring right ahead made him slow down and he stood on a cliff edge over which the peat-brown water cascaded in a mad frenzy down into the narrow glen.

Sky-lined he dropped behind a clump of heather. The glen was spread out below like a panorama. There was the loch and at its foot a whitewashed cottage. That would be Kerr's — the shepherd. Going from left to right in line with the beach was the jeep track. A harsh scar among the bright summer colours.

Six men were riding up the glen towards the waterfall. They were mounted on tough, little Highland garrons. Behind them a Land-Rover crawled along the track.

Six to one. He should run . . . but? They probably thought they were after one unharmed, frightened man. He had only a pistol and should run. Yet . . .

Kennedy was mistaken about the

hunters being cocksure. They had heard how he had slipped into the castle and out again. The Chief had warned that he was dangerous. But he had to be caught or killed at all costs.

The leader was a Rhodesian who had served his apprenticeship fighting as a mercenary in various African wars. Conflicts where prisoners were cut up for dog meat. He was still alive.

He did not like the way that the glen narrowed as they neared the head. There could be danger there. Under the falls the path swung away from the river and followed the line of cliffs to the moor above. Just short of the precipice he held up his hand. It looked okay but better to be sure.

'Connors, get up there and check it out.'

At the top, the horseman stood up in the stirrups and turned his head. Nothing but rocks and heather. He shouted the all clear and dismounted. Connors relaxed on a patch of smooth grass and lit a long cigar. He had a good ten minutes before the others arrived. He was unaware of the figure rising smoothly out of the heather behind him.

The cliff path was awkward even for the sure-footed garron. Exasperated, the Rhodesian reined in for a moment. A large object plummeted from above and hit the turf with a sodden thump in front of his beast. Brutally he brought the startled garron under control and slid from the saddle.

Connors lay on his back, his face contorted in his death agony. He had just time to realize his mistake when a 40 lb chunk of granite landed on top of his skull.

Shouting wildly, Kennedy pushed and threw the line of boulders he had collected down on the frantic men and animals below. Finally the last rock was despatched into space and he gazed down on the destruction below.

Connors and the Rhodesian had the company of one other on their journey to hell. The others were galloping pell-mell down the glen.

He wasted no time in gloating but collected Connors's sub-machine-gun and spare magazines before trotting back towards the sheltering hills.

But his luck had run out. For the remainder of the day he ran and hid, ran and hid. McRee handled his men with skill and cunning, never letting them walk into another ambush.

Using the helicopter as a forward scout, he drove the fugitive over the mountains. Only old skills still deep in his subconscious saved his skin time and again. Old tricks were remembered.

His earlier exhilaration collapsed like a pricked balloon. The continual running and scrambling over some of the roughest country in the world took toll of his physical resources. Only willpower and tenacity — and sheer bloody-mindedness — kept him going.

He felt like a pheasant being driven forward by beaters — the guns would not be too far ahead. Slowly and inevitably he was being flushed out and pushed towards Corrie As — a gigantic cliff lined gash cut out of the mountain whose Gaelic name translated as Peak of Eternity — apt, he thought wryly. He weaved from side to side and splashed through bogs that sucked at his boots. Once in that corrie he was done.

But lines of men kept coming between him and freedom. As he neared the corrie, the wind strengthened. The deep glen acted as a funnel sucking air down from the high tops. It gave him an idea that might gain him time — valuable time.

All pretence at hiding was thrown aside and he raced through the blue twilight into the mouth of the corrie. Breath rasping, he ran as he had never ran before. Shouts were raised behind him. Mouth open, he bounded over the carpet of heather for the cliffs ahead.

There, he wrenched out handfuls of dry grass. Fumbling with his lighter, he finally got the makeshift torch alight. A few shots spun off the rocks around him. Bending down he touched the heather at this feet with the flames and running a few yards did it again. A few more yards and again . . . and again.

The funnelled breeze caught the flames and drove them down the corrie towards his hunters. The belt of fire formed an impenetrable wall. Excited shouts turned to yells of terror.

He had got his time. Behind him the cliffs split. A steep shale slope filled the crack. The stones were loose and it was like climbing a wall of marbles. Two steps up and slide back three. Fate had given him a chance, but fate was not making it easy.

He dragged air into his lungs in short, painful gulps, but it was never enough. His sight blurred. Countless times he fell and heaved himself up with slashed and bleeding fingers.

Then he was lying on his face on sweet-smelling grass at the top. He crawled back to the cliff edge. Below was a burning pit of hell. The whole glen was ablaze end to end.

Like a bolt of white lightning, a shaft of light swept along the shale. It was the chopper. The roaring of the wind whirling about him had covered the sound of its rotors as it lifted over the ridge. It hovered level with Kennedy about two hundred yards out.

It shook and shuddered. The pilot was either very good or very mad to bring his aircraft so low over Corrie As. The down-draught threatened to snatch it out of the sky.

This was the sod who had harried him all day. Kennedy felt a deep hatred for the pilot nice and clean in his warm plane. While he was tired, dirty, frightened and running.

He pushed the sub-machine-gun into his shoulder and let off the whole magazine at the hovering shadow. Ripping out the empty, he slammed in another. Suddenly he was pinned in the centre of the tunnel of light. Blinded he fired wildly into the air. Bullets thudded into the grass around him. There could only be one end to this uneven battle. He flinched waiting for smashing lead to tear him apart.

With a burst of power the helicopter started to lift away.

Red-hot wind seared his face as bullets whipped past it . . . from behind! He whirled round. McRee leaned nonchalantly on a shepherd's crook a few yard away. Two others covered him with rifles.

The clear voice carried well despite the wind and the sound of the departing helicopter. 'Be a good chap and drop that gun. I don't want to kill you. Not just yet anyway.'

9

The trapped reporter tried to remember how many shots he had fired at the helicopter. He was certain that one burst remained in the magazine. But if he was wrong . . .

He ignored the two armed men. This was between him and McRee.

'Come on, Kennedy, you are finished. Drop the gun. It is empty anyway.'

Kennedy gave a harsh, strained laugh. 'Then why ask me to drop it? You are not sure, are you? I have one burst left and I am keeping it all for you.'

'You would be dead before you could pull the trigger.'

Kennedy felt outside his body as if watching the clifftop drama from the sidelines. Fleetingly he wondered if a condemned man facing an execution squad felt the same. But while he hung onto the gun, he had a bargaining point.

'I am not so sure, McRee. I have seen

men with three or four bullets in them still fight. Sure I will get it — but I might have time to blow your bloody head off.'

McRee tapped the turf with his crook. His sure conceit seemed to have slipped a mite and there was confusion on the faces of the others.

Then one of the gunmen grunted and pointed to the sky. The helicopter was returning and by the sound of the engine something was wrong. The smooth buzzing had become a shrieking, metal-tearing rattle. The black shadow flew like a lumbering black beetle.

It was shaking itself apart. Out of control it began to turn in tight circles. Apparently the pilot was trying to reach some flat ground near them. But the plane was doomed.

A tiny figure detached itself from the chopper. The passenger was taking a chance. He risked serious injury, but it was a chance. He was unlucky. The engine noise drowned his despairing scream as he missed the edge of the cliff by inches and plunged into the blazing cauldron below.

A final screech of protest and the motor stopped. The sudden silence was intense.

The machine dropped out of the sky, tumbling over and over. It smashed on to the shale slope and with a whoosh blew up. The blazing fuselage rolled over and over scattering burning wreckage. Long ribbons of flaming aviation fuel licked out over the stones. Then it hit the bottom and blew apart in a final explosion.

McRee's handsome features were Satanic in the red glare. The other two were staring in horror into the corrie.

This was Kennedy's chance. Smoothly he swung the sub-machine-gun up to line on the Chief's chest. The hawkish face twisted in fear.

He pressed the trigger. There was only one bullet left. As the weapon jerked in his hands one of the gunmen leapt forward — right into the line of fire. The 9 mm slug lifted him up and almost gently dropped him over the edge of the precipice. He did not have time to start screaming.

Kennedy turned and fled into the darkening night. A heavy punch on the shoulder drove him forward on to his knees. Scrambling up, he staggered on.

There was no pain but he knew that would come later. A warmth spread down his left side and his vision began to go. There was shouting behind him. He had to find a place to hide.

With a frightened yelp he stepped over a small cliff and fell about six feet, fortunately into soft sand bordering a meandering burn. A lance of agony slashed at his shoulder. He was in a narrow gorge only a few feet across. He crawled deeper into it. At a bend the water had carved out a small cave. Breathing hard he pulled himself into it on his elbows.

The fine silver granite sand was soft and dry and he lay back with a sigh. He could rest here. When the full blackness of night covered the land he would move on. But first he would have to see to that wound. He must . . .

The wind's banshee howling brought him round. It had risen to gale force and was trumpeting through the narrow gorge. His watch told him he had been out for about two hours.

It was as black as the Earl of Hell's boots. No stars could be glimpsed through the break in the walls above him. The air was warm, but when he breathed he could taste the moisture in it. The atmosphere throbbed with a sort of life of its own. By the feel of things this storm was going to be a beauty.

A gnawing pain spread over his chest and up his neck. His shirt and anorak were stiff with dried blood. Gently his fingers explored the injury. The bullet had torn a gash across the top of his shoulder. It was messy but the bleeding had stopped. It was not dangerous — if seen soon by a doctor. Clumsily he folded a handkerchief and pressed it over the ragged flesh.

Tremendously thirsty, he dipped his flushed face into the burn's cool water and drank deeply. He let the clean freshness soak into his skin.

With an immense effort he heaved himself up. Violent shivering racked his frame and shambling over the sand he climbed out of the gorge. A line of torches only a couple of hundred yards away was bobbing in his direction.

Turning, he lumbered away through the bracken. The wind had dropped to a whisper. There was a not unpleasant tingling that tickled his scalp. But he was barely aware of it. His whole concentration was directed to placing one foot in front of another.

Lightning ripped the black carpet above him. The deep resounding bellow of thunder shook the very rocks. The hunters stopped and stared up filled with a primeval fear. The wind grew until its wailing made speech impossible. Heavy clouds collided with the mountains and emptied themselves on the land below.

Rainwater streamed over stone slabs and down corries and gullies. Tiny burns rose in minutes to raging torrents. And continuously the wind screamed like a thousand blood-crazed dervishes.

McRee and his followers huddled helplessly behind the boulders and beneath overhanging cliffs. Nature had gone wild and taken over the hills.

The fugitive lumbered and tottered

through the tempest. The thunder went unheard, drowned by the mad thumping of his own heart. The downpour mixed with salty sweat and blood from his reopened wound flowed down over his chest.

His mind had withdrawn into itself. The real world no longer interested him — it could only hurt. Like a wounded animal, he swayed and weaved along the line of least resistance. His lurching path led downwards. His boots hit a path and turned along it. A dozen times he fell and a dozen times he pushed himself up. His bent figure dragged itself on.

His way reached up over a ridge and down into a deep glen. The crazy, stumbling figure was protected by the thick curtain of rain.

A moment of near sanity returned when he found himself stumbling along the jeep track that circled the island. A last fragment of reason warned him to get off the bulldozed path. Dragging his feet, he crossed the machair that bordered the beach. High, fierce, white-topped waves slammed down on the sand and hurtled towards him.

He stood there, wounded and blind, like a fighting bull before the final deadly thrust. For the first time his instincts did not know what to do. His spirit was at the end of its tether. His body could take no more punishment.

The wind was the final straw. It tore at his tattered clothes with clawing fingers. It slapped and punched his flinching body. A tremendous gust smashed against his back and he crumpled on the wet grass. His cheek slammed against a sharp flint and split open.

The stinging pain got through and he opened his eyes for a moment. Glaring white light from a patrolling Land-Rover swept over a mound just ahead. He forced his expended muscles to one last effort. Just a few feet into the waving bracken. His head hung like a thrashed dog's. One hand slid forward into nothing and he tumbled into a narrow tunnel. Like a beast returning to its lair to die, he dragged himself into the still darkness.

Kennedy floated to the surface like a submariner escaping from his sunken boat lying in the great depths where sunlight never reaches. Leisurely at first, then with ever-increasing speed, he came up out of unconsciousness. He fought against but finally surrendered to the pull and broke surface.

He was naked and in a comfortable bed. Fresh linen sheets were smooth and cool against his skin. His shoulder beat with a dull ache. There was the delightful scent of smouldering peat. The storm had abated and someone was humming a pleasant Hebridean melody.

He opened his eyes. Above were smoke-blackened timbers supporting a low roof of thatch. An old woman wrapped in a red tartan shawl sat in a high-backed chair before the fire. A table scrubbed white, a polished chest of drawers and large cupboard made up the rest of the furniture. A watery sun shone through small windows in the thick whitewashed walls.

The slight movement of his head caught her attention. 'Awake, are you?' Her voice was soft and throaty, more used to the lilting Gaelic than the harsh English tongue.

'Where am I and how did I get here?' croaked Kennedy.

'You could say that you just dropped in!' Her laugh was the tinkling of a gurgling stream over round stones. 'I am Mrs Grant — Mrs Mary Grant.'

He attempted to lift himself up on one elbow. But, with a sudden cry, fell back.

'That serves you right, young man. You are quite safe here, so lie back and rest. You did a lot of talking when you were asleep. And I have guessed of your trouble with the Chief. But you are safe here.'

She shuffled over to the bed. She was an incredibly old and dignified woman. Sharp eyes scrutinized him closely. Brown hands folded in front of the long grey woollen dress.

A small smile curved his lips. 'I was only worried about your reputation, Mrs Grant. What would the ladies of Inverawe say if they found you with a naked man in your bed?'

'You are definitely on the mend. Now you must have something to eat.'

It was just after noon. While she

prepared the food, she answered his questions.

Very early that morning she had been watching the storm when she had heard groaning from behind the tall cupboard.

'From behind the cupboard?' he gasped incredulously.

She nodded with a smile. The back wall was built into the mound he had stumbled across. The cupboard was designed to swing away from the wall on hidden hinges. Behind a tunnel led to a central chamber.

'It sounds like a prehistoric burial chamber,' declared her patient. The archaeologists back at the hotel had said there were a few on the island.

She did not know anything about that, but in her great grandfather's time the Excise man would have been very interested in what had been hidden there.

He had been raving but had managed to crawl to the bed. There she had stripped and washed him.

The colour rose in his pale ravaged face. Tritely she told him that she had been married for forty years before losing her man and had been brought up with five brothers. Then she had stitched and dressed the wound. In her young days there had been no doctor on the island. Injuries were treated at home. A length of fine fishing-gut for the stitching and green mould from an old loaf of bread for the dressing.

He turned his head in sudden alarm to examine the neat bandage.

'Don't worry, it works,' she snapped tartily. 'I also gave you a herb potion to ease the pain and make you sleep.'

For the first time he realized that his head was clear and there was no sign of fever. He felt rested and except for a dull throbbing suffered little discomfort. Suddenly he remembered the hunt. Her age would not protect her from McRee's rage if he was found here.

'That was a bullet wound,' he said uneasily. 'McRee wants me dead. He is an evil man.'

She pushed her head forward like an angry hen. 'I know that. I will help you in any way I can. And Angus Kerr will be here soon because of the storm. He will want to see that I am all right. The silly man thinks I am too old to care for myself. But he will know what to do.'

He let his head fall back on the pillow. 'You don't like McRee?'

Mrs Grant had met him only once. He had arrived at her door one afternoon and offered to buy her cottage. She had turned him down although the offer had been more than generous.

The Chief had been furious.

'The Devil wa looking out of his eyes. That man has a black soul.'

He ate the broth that the old woman had made and fell into a deep sleep.

A well-polished brass oil-lamp filled the room with a soft light when he awoke. The sun had just dipped behind the hills. The room was empty. His clothes washed and mended lay at the foot of the bed. He had just finished dressing when Mrs Grant returned with a tall elderly man in heavy tweeds.

Kerr had a full open face tanned a deep brown more by hill winds than by the sun. Grey eyes were keen with that slightly unfocussed look of a man used to

155

looking into far distances.

The shepherd stamped over to the fire. He pulled out a stubby black pipe and packed it with what seemed to be tarry rope. When he had it pulling to his satisfaction and clouds of blue smoke floated up to hover beneath the thatch, he spoke briefly and directly.

'Why is the Chief after you?'

Kennedy told him quickly all that had happened over the last few days. 'But help should arrive from the mainland in the next twenty-four hours.'

Angus Kerr accepted a cup of tea from the old woman. The fine cup looked like a thimble in his huge, rough hands. He told the reporter that he had had suspicions about the Chief for some time.

'Take that Adventure School. Most of the young men who go there are fine enough lads and I am sure that it does them a lot of good. But every now and then there is an older group. They are too hard-eyed for my liking and they never stray far from the tower. No trekking over the hills for them. There is a crowd like that there just now.'

The shepherd rose and stretched. It was time to start. He believed McRee suspected his prey was in these parts.

'There are more men than midges about here. Sooner or later they will come here, I am sure. We will cross the hills to my place.'

Kennedy shrugged. He was in the shepherd's hands. But could they slip through the searchers?

Kerr spat in the fire with contempt. 'I crossed this afternoon in bright sunlight and they still didn't see me!'

The reporter turned to thank the old lady whose skill, kindness and courage had saved him. He put his good arm round her bent shoulders and squeezed gently.

She reached out and touched the slung sub-machine-gun. 'That man has brought death and violence to our island. His soul belongs to the Devil. Give the Devil back his own!'

The tempest of the previous night might never have been. A warm wind caressed them as they climbed away from the sea.

As a lesson in crossing enemy held territory at night, it was a masterpiece. Kerr used every advantage the layout of the country offered. Folds in the ground, deep shadows in glens and under cliffs, hidden paths through bogs . . . all the time heading west. Once he waved his charge down and they crawled on their bellies for three hundred yards through a maze of rocks. It was not until he picked up the smell of cigarette smoke that Kennedy guessed why.

He had believed that his own service training and experience had made him an expert in this sort of work, but alongside Kerr he was a rank amateur.

Kerr kept heading towards where the sun had gone down with that shepherd's stride that ate up the miles. His only concession to his age and Kennedy's weakened state was to stop now and then and lean on his crook.

They crossed a ridge and the journalist could smell the sea. No torches bobbed or swayed below them. The ocean sparkled under the stars and was empty of shipping. The regular flash of a distant lighthouse flickered on the horizon.

'Seems clear,' commented Kennedy. The strain was beginning to tell on him.

'It does that. But we will still go canny.'

Kennedy rolled over on his elbow and looked up at his new friend. 'Where did you learn to evade the enemy like that? I know you are familiar with these hills but to avoid men set on killing you — that is something different.'

There was a harsh laugh in the night. 'Och, you young men are all the same! Old men ken nothing. I learned to survive in the First War. There were only two types of soldiers in France. Those who learned to survive — and the dead ones. Survival was more important than killing.

'Except for the big pushes, most of the fighting was done at night in no-man's-land. You had to be good to stay alive.'

Kennedy gasped to himself. This man who had crossed these hills with the skill and strength of a mountain goat must have been well over eighty years old!

10

Kennedy sank gratefully into an old armchair. The last couple of miles down the glen to the shepherd's home nearly proved too much for him. Kerr passed him a cigarette and the nicotine assaulted his brain and his head spun.

'Now we deserve a dram — whisky or vodka?'

The newspaperman inspected the bottles. The whisky was a clear lustrous amber in a lemonade bottle. He wondered what illicit still it had come from. The label on the vodka bottle was in angular Russian script. He had a feeling that neither spirit had ever come under the examination of a Customs officer. He selected the whisky.

The craggy hillman caught him eyeing the vodka. Russian fishing-boats sometimes anchored offshore. They liked whisky — so they swapped.

'This bottle I got the other day. There are some in the area just now. I also suspect they help themselves to the odd sheep, but I can't prove it.'

Kennedy's professional instincts told him there was more to it than just that. Smuggling most probably — and not just the odd bottle. But he did not push it.

The shepherd produced a bachelor's meal of thick beef sandwiches and pint mugs of strong black tea. After eating, Kennedy dropped into a deep sleep with a cigarette still between his fingers. The old man gently withdrew it and then quietly left the room.

The birds were greeting the false dawn when he came to. Although he had only been asleep for a couple of hours he felt refreshed.

Kerr stood with his back to the empty fireplace. His pipe stuck out from his tight lips like a battering ram and the grey eyes glowed in the light of the oil lamp.

'What now?' he growled. There was a nervousness about him that worried the journalist.

'I told you at Mrs Grant's,' said Kennedy quickly. 'Any time now my boss will get things moving and soon Inverawe will be swarming with police. But you obviously have something on your mind. Why don't you spit it out?'

While Kennedy had been sleeping, the shepherd had gone out to scout around. He had been walking along the track when a Land-Rover had driven up and stopped. The driver had been that fellow Jamieson.

'Morning, Kerr. You are up early.'

'I am always up early. Usually I never meet anybody, but this morning I keep bumping into your people. They are all over the hills. What is up?'

'There are some deer poachers about,' replied Jamieson glibly. 'From the mainland. The Chief wants them caught. Seen any strangers about?'

Naturally Kerr claimed that he had not. But that he would be going into town later and would keep his eyes open.

The sun had not yet cleared the hills and it was still dark on the road. Kerr could only see the driver clearly. But as the vehicle moved off someone in the back began to whistle 'A Gordon For Me'. He only got out a couple of bars when he stopped suddenly as if a hand had been slapped over his mouth.

The old shepherd ran a rough hand over his face. 'John at the hotel served in the Gordon Highlanders in the last war and often whistled that tune. I would stake my life that he was a prisoner in that vehicle!'

It had been heading towards the tower.

Kennedy walked back and forth across the room. He guessed what had happened. Somehow John had tried to make the mainland. McRee had suspected what he was up to and picked him up. He could not be left in Jamieson's hands!

But Angus Kerr thought that any attempt at rescue would end in disaster. It was one thing giving the slip to a bunch of amateurs in the wilderness. But to get John out of that tower — that was another matter.

Kennedy ruminated on the problem for a couple of minutes. The bud of an idea blossomed into full flower. The shepherd saw him smile — it was not a nice smile and he felt sorry for what Jamieson was about to receive.

A hot sun had burned away the mist from the high peaks. Only a few wisps remained in the depths of deep black corries. The Land-Rover bumped slowly over the rough track. The storm had torn it up quite a bit. The driver and his mate had been up all night circling the island on the look out for the fugitive and their eyes burned with exhaustion. Even fear of their leader could not stop their brains becoming dull and tired.

The vehicle rounded a bend to find Kerr waving them down.

'What the hell does the old bugger want?' grumbled the driver. His companion slid his sub-machine-gun out of sight under a blanket.

'What is it, Kerr?'

The shepherd seemed frightened and kept glancing over his shoulder.

'Mr Jamieson told me earlier that you are searching for poachers. Well I have just spotted a stranger.'

Both men scrambled out and the driver grabbed Kerr by the lapels. 'Where, man? Where did you see him?'

The driver stiffened. He tried to speak

but his throat was blocked with fear. A cold round circle pressed against his head just an inch behind his ear.

'Right here,' snarled Kennedy savagely. 'Now both of you drop your trousers. You can't do much harm with them round your ankles.'

He ordered them to lie down and searched the Land-Rover, discovering the other weapon. He smacked a full magazine into his empty gun with a relieved sigh.

'Now, old man, get into the ditch. I can't leave you about to tell any of their pals about this.'

The captives heard the beginning of a cry that bubbled off into nothing. Kennedy appeared before them cleaning a hunting-knife with a handful of grass.

'Get up. You are going to give me a lift to the tower.'

As the Land-Rover vanished round a bend, the shepherd's contorted body rolled out of the ditch. He stood up and retrieved a game-bag and shotgun from behind a boulder. Kennedy had refused to take him along and insisted on this little act in case his rescue attempt went wrong.

'It will protect you from McRee,' he said.

Kennedy had no difficulty getting the two men to talk. They confirmed what he had already guessed about the little barman. The information came bubbling out in an uncontrolled rush.

The Chief had stopped the ferry sailing from the island after the reporter had escaped. It had been put out that the ship had broken down. The barman had been caught trying to take a small motor boat.

'We just carry out orders,' babbled a very frightened driver.

How many men were at the tower?

Words fell from their mouths. Jamieson and five others. 'That's the truth,' sobbed the driver. 'God help me!'

'I don't know if the Almighty will. I know I won't.' Venom flowed from the cold green eyes. Something within Kennedy had switched off. He was now as much a killer as McRee.

The Land-Rover braked just out of sight of the tower. He ordered the two men into the back and securely tied them up with insulating tape from the tool-kit.

Then he crept to where he could see the track sweep down to the ancient building. The squat tower was exactly as his researches back in the city had described it. There was one entrance on the seaward side. Kerr had told him that the kitchen and visitors' accommodation was on the ground floor. A tall wireless aerial rose from the roof. There was another narrow entrance on the landward side where the track passed beneath the walls.

Trotting back to the vehicle, he started it up and gave his prisoners an icy smile. 'We are going for a drive — a very short one!'

Their eyes bulged and their heels beat against the metal floor as the Land-Rover quickly picked up speed.

'Must leave you now,' yelled Kennedy and jumped out into a deep bed of heather.

He raised his head just in time to watch the vehicle sail on over a steep cliff. In the sudden silence he could hear the waves slopping on the beach for a second. Then a deep explosion followed by a plume of red-tinged smoke surging up over the cliff edge shattered the peace of the morning.

'Now ask God for help,' he whispered. 'You'll be meeting him soon!'

Men tumbled out of the tower. He could hear their alarmed shouts as they scrambled down to the burning wreckage.

Leaping up, he ran like a bat out of hell to the tower. He risked a glance through the open door and saw a long empty hall with doors leading off it ending in a flight of stairs. He scurried along the passage-way, gun barrel swinging left and right. Pausing at the stairs he listened — only a heavy silence.

His thick rubber soles made little sound as he padded up the stone stairs. The door at the end was ajar and he looked into a small vaulted hall. At the far end Jamieson was staring out of a window.

He stepped softly in. The hall was deserted and he lined his weapon up on Jamieson's spine.

The man raised his head slightly as if he had heard something and turned slowly. No flicker of surprise disturbed his bearded face, but his eyes narrowed and glinted dangerously.

The reporter's finger took up first pressure on the trigger. A twitch and he would smear the man's belly all over the stone wall.

'Don't do it, Kennedy! One of my chaps is in the minstrel gallery right above you and his gun is pointing at the top of your skull. I would like to see the effect of a full magazine of bullets being pumped vertically into you. Would they come out of your backside?'

Five long seconds ticked by as Kennedy held the eyes of McRee's number-one man. Was the man bluffing? No, he was too confident. He could take the big bastard with him but it was the Chief he wanted.

Gradually he let the machine-gun barrel drop and finally opened his fingers to let it fall at his feet.

A sigh escaped Jamieson. 'For a second you had me really worried.' Taking a pistol from his belt, he waved at the window. 'Come over here and admire the view.'

A figure floated face down in the water

about two hundred yards out. Slowly the air trapped in the clothing escaped and it slid beneath the waves. But Kennedy had recognized the white jacket.

'Another tragic accident,' said Jamieson. 'And now there is a vacancy for a barman at the hotel.'

Kennedy slumped into a chair. His hands shook and his muscles quivered like violin strings. He tried to keep his face impassive but the corner of his mouth twitched. Another good man dead and because of him.

A tall youngster ran into the hall. His good-looking face was twisted in anger. 'Evans and White were in the Land-Rover,' he gabbled out. 'And it wasn't an accident. They were tied up in the back and we had to watch them burn to death. We could do nothing. It was horrible.'

Jamieson shrugged with disinterest. 'They were fools, Grey!' He turned to his prisoner. 'Your work?'

The reporter managed a grin.

Grey leapt forward and swung a hard fist into his face. He slithered into a senseless heap on the floor.

When he came round he was back in the chair. Grey was at one side obviously eager to finish what he had started. Jamieson came through the door. He had been in touch with McRee by radio and the prisoner had to be taken to the castle.

'He wants to deal with you himself. Grey bring a vehicle round to the door.'

Kennedy felt sick and light-headed and could not stop a giggle.

The big man stared down at him. 'What's so funny?'

'You! This is turning into a second-rate 1940s movie. Can't you see that you are all washed up? There has been too much killing. The police know I am here and will come looking. Your only chance is to get out — now.'

Jamieson towered over him. 'You may be right at that. But McRee will either have a contingency plan to handle you or a nice safe way of getting out of the country.'

Grey appeared at the double. 'Sir. That American is approaching the tower — on a bloody horse!'

Jamieson cursed. 'How the hell did he

get past our patrols? Get back to the burning car. And you, Kennedy, shut up. One peep and Carson gets it too.'

In spite of his predicament, Kennedy could not keep back a smile. Carson was fitted out in high-heeled boots, tight blue jeans and hip-length canvas jacket. As he entered the hall he pulled off a well worn Stetson and slapped non-existent dust from his pants.

'Hi there. McRee said I could drop in for a look-see.' His soft eyes swept the room and settled on Kennedy. 'What the hell happened to you? Someone's husband catch up on you?'

Jamieson interrupted to say that the reporter had been in an accident. 'You may have seen the smoke. He was lucky to have escaped with his life.'

The tall Highlander offered the visitor a drink and also handed one to his prisoner with a warning glare.

Over the whisky Carson explained that he had borrowed a horse at one of the farms and gone for a ride in the hills. When he had spotted the tower, he had decided to drop in. But now he had to head back to Inverawe.

The high heels rapped loudly on the wooden floor as he strolled across the room. 'Sorry I can't give you a lift, Davie boy. But that poor damned horse finds it difficult enough to carry me.'

The battered Kennedy felt a shock when he raised his head in farewell. The innocent blue eyes had darkened to the colour of gun-metal. Hard and piercing, they flashed a danger signal.

'Watch yourself, Davie. You don't want another accident.' The slow drawl had vanished and the voice was clipped and decisive.

Carson stumped over to the door. His eyes bored into the seated reporter. The atmosphere was suddenly pregnant with menace.

Kennedy swung his eyes up to the threatening barrel protruding from the gallery. The black spout was pointing directly at his chest. It looked as large as a fifteen-inch naval gun.

The American halted beneath the gallery. He reached under his jacket and smoothly drew out a huge Colt .45. He pumped two bullets into the ornamental woodwork above his head. The hidden gunman was lifted up by the powerful bullets and draped across the balustrade. Blood poured from his open mouth in a scarlet flood.

Carson swung the revolver on the shocked Jamieson. 'Reach.'

Kennedy felt his heart suddenly go like a steam-hammer. He snatched up his sub-machine-gun from where his captor had kicked it behind a curtain. 'Who the hell are you?'

'I'm the good guy in the white hat.' Outside the faint sound of shots could be heard. 'And if I'm right that's some of the guys in the black hats getting theirs.'

He stepped aside as running steps could be heard on the stairs. Grey skidded halfway down the hall in a swirl of tartan.

'We have been ambushed down at the Land-Rover. I managed to get clear. What will we do?' Panic was clear in his shrill plea.

Jamieson's bearded features were blue with anger and disgust. The younger man's mouth dropped as he saw his boss with his hands in the air. His head swivelled in slow motion. The American and Kennedy covered him.

His desperate eyes were drawn to the mess of blood on the floor and the two straight lines where he had skidded through it. He lifted his face to the dead hanging gunman.

With an almost animal growl, he threw himself at the reporter. There were two barks and smoke spiralled from the revolver and the sub-machine-gun. The two slugs left little of his head.

'That lad was too mean to live,' murmured Kennedy. He whirled as another figure entered the room.

Angus Kerr handled his shotgun with long familiarity. His face had the steadfastness of an Old Testament prophet.

'You will have no trouble with the others. They are either dead or running like hell!'

11

A few seconds and Kennedy had the whole story. Kerr had been on his way to Inverawe to check that Isla Armstrong was safe when he had met Carson. The American had just left her an hour earlier and she was fine.

'Angus and I decided that the first priority was to give you a hand,' said Carson.

They had arrived just in time to witness him doing his bit towards cutting down the island's traffic problem. When he did not reappear from the tower after a few minutes, they guessed he had met trouble.

'So we agreed to do the 7th Cavalry bit. I would ride up like a dumb tourist. He would stay under cover and do nothing while I tried to get you out without fuss.'

The shepherd took over. 'Then I heard the shooting and dealt with those outside,' he grunted briefly. He handed over Kennedy's small haversack. He had found it where the reporter had hidden it before his one man assault on the ancient stronghold. The parcel he had brought up from Glasgow was still in it.

'Let's find John and get away from this place,' went on the shepherd.

'John is dead,' said Kennedy flatly and explained how he had been killed.

Jamieson stood stiff and erect. His eyes were empty, but the stiffness of his jaw betrayed his choler and tension.

'What the hell is going on anyway?' demanded the American.

'I haven't time to explain now. But McRee is mixed up in a rotten business and is responsible for a good few killings. Now you keep an eye on this bastard here. Kerr come with me. I want to look over this place.'

It would be a waste of time questioning their prisoner. He might be a ruthless killer but he had guts. Even with the big revolver threatening him the man showed no sign of fear.

Most of the building was as he

expected an Adventure Training School to be. Dining-room, kitchen, sleeping-accommodation, rest-rooms and stores packed with climbing equipment etc. The staff quarters revealed a large radio — the link with McRee.

'A bit big that, just for keeping in touch with the boss at Inverawe,' commented the shepherd with a frown.

Roughly hewn steps took them down to the ancient cellars. All the rooms were open except one. A heavy padlock held the thick door secure. Two bullets soon solved the problem.

The low room was stacked high with heavy wooden and metal boxes. They had a familiar look to the two ex-servicemen. From somewhere the countryman produced a screwdriver.

'Phew!' breathed Kennedy as he raised a lid. Kerr opened three more. The reporter perched on the corner of one of the open boxes and reached for a cigarette — but changed his mind.

They were surrounded by enough small arms and ammunition to equip an army. There were also supplies of various explosives. It must have cost a fortune and been smuggled into the country.

'The IRA?' suggested Kerr.

Kennedy shook his head. He knew the explanation was much simpler than that. He told the shepherd to take some of the arms upstairs where he would join him soon. Then took the brown paper parcel from the haversack.

He met Kerr coming out of the kitchen carrying a bulging bag. They would need food before this was all over.

A shot echoed from above and they bounded up the stairs to the hall to find Carson hauling himself off the floor. 'The son of a bitch suckered me. He ran through that door in the corner.'

A circular staircase wound up to a trapdoor which was locked. Above it was the roof of the tower. Jamieson was as safe as if he was relaxing in the Chief's drawing-room at the castle.

The reporter turned to Kerr. Did he know of any place they could hide out for a while?

The old man had just the place. 'The Customs and Excise men could never find it, so this lot won't.'

'Just one thing,' interrupted the American. And with a length of wire secured the trapdoor from their side. 'We don't want him getting down too soon.'

Kennedy could never say what made him leap out of the door on to the track. Except that his instinct for danger was at its highest level. A huge block of faced granite smashed into the ground behind him.

'God! That bugger never gives up,' he growled admiringly spraying the parapet with bullets while his friends jumped to safety.

Obscene curses and threats followed them up the track. At the top of the rise he halted and stared back. 'I would take cover if I were you,' he advised.

'Why?' muttered Carson. 'There is no time to waste. Let's keep moving.'

'McRee tried to have me blown up in Glasgow. The bomb was in that haversack of mine. I left it down in the arms store and lit the blue touch-paper!'

The trio dived behind some scattered boulders. Jamieson's tall figure was clear against the sky. He gave a defiant wave of his fist.

The ground beneath them suddenly rolled like an ocean swell and a grumbling rumble resounded out of the earth. Splendid flowers of red flame sprouted from the slim arrow slits. But the thick walls of the six-hundred-year-old fortress that had withstood English cannon contained the vast explosion in its bowels. They acted like the barrel of a gun and directed the full force of the cataclysm upwards towards the heavens . . . and Jamieson!

A tremendous stream of fire ruptured the roof to scar the lovely morning sky. A huge scarlet blasphemy that twisted and turned. At the peak a tiny figure seemed to hover for a second, then plunged down into the hell boiling within the tower.

The cave was spacious and dry. It faced the grey rolling Atlantic. Waves tumbled over pebbles to within a yard or so of the mouth. It was at the head of a cliff-lined half-moon bay. Smoke trickled up from a driftwood fire to vanish through cracks in the roof.

Carson soaked his feet in a rocky pool with an expression of sublime contentment.

The newspaperman had been watching him for some time. In his own way he was as big a mystery as his fellow countryman. A seemingly ordinary businessman, he had proved a very tough customer indeed.

He gave a rather old-fashioned cough. 'Carson, before we decide our next step, I think you should tell us why you dealt yourself in? Businessmen in Scotland don't go calling with Colt .45s.'

The American stared at the ground for a moment or so before replying. His name really was Richard Carson, and he was a partner in a firm that designed small marine engines — but only a sleeping partner. His brother ran it from a New England seaport. He himself was based in Las Vegas where he was boss of a private detective agency.

Some months ago he had received a letter from a Scottish cop — Sergeant George Campbell. Would he look into the background of a certain Roderick McRee?

'That was easy. McRee had been a well-known figure in the city. He had been in hotels and gambling. And we had all read of how he had sold up and come to Scotland as Chief of his clan.'

On the surface McRee had been straight — no criminal tie-ups. But there had been some rumours about hot money being passed in his joints. Nothing was ever proved though.

The private detective sent off his report and bill. A few weeks passed and a letter arrived from a Glasgow solicitor settling the account and explaining that his client had been drowned in an accident at Bargrennan.

But the cop's death bothered him. He had asked for a run-down on McRee. Then died only spitting distance from McRee's new home. It smelled.

His brother had been talking of taking a business trip to England for some time. Carson went instead. It was an ideal cover.

'I drove north and came over here. I made a few inquiries but turned up nothing sinister. But I did get an order for our engines!' he added with a touch of satisfaction.

'Then you arrived and things began to hum. I had intended to keep on the sidelines, but here am I hiding out like a bloody outlaw.'

Kennedy quickly explained his part in the drama. 'McRee is involved in something really big and I have an idea what it is — but cannot prove it yet.'

He told the others to get some rest and he would stand watch. He needed time to think.

He crunched over the pebbles and settled down on a patch of sea-washed turf. The sun was low on the horizon and he felt drained of verve and drive. McRee and his iniquities seemed of small importance as he let the sun's warmth soak into his face. His shoulder was throbbing painfully again.

Thinking did not come easily. The wheels of his mind were stiff and rusty. His head fell forward and the whisper of the waves and wind were soft in his ears. He wondered about Isla, but she was only a dim, shadowy figure. He slept.

The scraping of steel boot-nails on granite wrenched him from a dreamless slumber. The fire was a bed of white ash. The sun — an eye searing golden orb — was about to quench itself in the west. Kerr bent his knees and crouched down with concern showing on his stern face.

'I feel awful,' confessed Kennedy wryly. He felt confused and worried. 'We can't keep running. I think we should hole up here until help arrives from the mainland.'

Kerr's eyes were soft and his voice thoughtful and reasoned. 'You are exhausted, David, or you would not talk like that. You ken very well that there will be no help from over the water. The ferry is not running, the telephone line is cut and they will be watching for boats trying to cross.

'By the time your city friends get around to investigating we will be dead. And when McRee gets us he can cover up our deaths easily. The people in Inverawe don't ken what is going on.

'All he has to say is that we were visiting the tower and unfortunately some explosives left over from the track building blew up. And who would doubt the word of the Chief of the Clan McRee?

'We are on our own and have only one chance — get McRee!'

Kennedy scrambled up. It was an outrageous suggestion. The Chief would have the town and castle covered from all angles. And there were only three of them. It was mad.

'As it is I should never have got you involved.'

'Why? Just because I am an old man who has spent most of his life in the hills wi' his sheep? You forget I have seen more violence and death than McRee and all his men put together.

'And then there is Inverawe. Just because it only merits one policeman does not mean that the men don't know how to fight. Those nice decent fisher-men, farmers, clerks and grocers have been commandos, paratroops and High-land infantrymen in their time. When they learn the truth they will help.'

Kennedy stared blindly at the ocean. The man was right. They joined the American at the cave. Did he want to hide or fight?

'I never did like sitting waiting for it.

Let's go out and give it to the bastards!'

Kennedy grinned and shook his head. 'Well that makes it unanimous, but we are all crazy.'

But how to get through the hills to the town? The Chief would have every available man out searching. Kerr might make it — but not lumbered with the other two men.

The shepherd was watching a fishing-boat two or three miles out. 'I will look after that. I have an idea where I can get some help.' The craggy hillman smiled slyly and strode into the gathering darkness.

Only a faint yellow line marked the horizon as the sun bid a last farewell. Stars sparkled in the deep purple roof above them. But above the hills they were going out one by one as a layer of low cloud swept over the island. The sea had retreated from the cave as if following the sun on its travels. There was a chill in the soft wind.

Carson huddled over the fire, his thin desert blood unused to the cold nights of the north.

The reporter stood outside and felt the dew settling on his hair. Where had the shepherd got to? He had been away too long.

His first task on taking up position had been to survey the immediate area about him. He carefully scrutinized every rock and bush. Later in the depths of night, they would take on another mould. That gorse bush above the cave — to a nervous man it could become a crouching man about to leap. That washed up log twenty yards away. It would be easy to convince one's self that it was a hunter crawling over the stones. He had stood guard before — the most lonely and frightening task in the world.

After he was sure that he had labelled every rock and bush, he closed his eyes and listened. He catalogued every sound. The slip slop of water on pebbles. The gurgle and protest of the retreating tide. Stones grinding together as the water sucked them from their beds. Bracken rustling in the wind. Each sound was indexed and recorded in his memory.

A shape or sound that did not have a

place in this index would bring him to one hundred per cent alertness. Once it was identified as harmless, he would relax again.

The last pale trace of the sun had gone when he suddenly felt uneasy. Something disturbed him. He did not know what, but something had broken the pattern. He probed the cliffs and beach as the likely danger points. A low cry brought Carson to his side.

He never looked directly at an object, but slightly to the side of it. Even an experienced man staring directly at an object in the dark could sometimes swear it moved. There was nothing wrong that he could pin down. All the time his ears were taking in and throwing aside diagnosed sounds.

His hair tingled. There was something out there. His eyes glittered in the fading starlight as he swung them over the ground again. Nothing!

The breeze freshened a little. There it was — a pulsating throb! Turning his head from side to side, he tried to identify it. The sound was coming from seawards.

The green eyes ached as they tried to pierce the wall of blackness. Then there it was — a darker shadow about one hundred yards out. A small motor-boat had entered the bay.

Nudging Carson, he pointed and slipped the safety-catch of his weapon. They crouched in the night shadows waiting.

A few yards out the engine was switched off and the craft drifted in to ground on the beach. Two men jumped out and pulled it up out of reach of the tide. Then they strode confidently into the cave.

With weapons ready at their hips, Kennedy and Carson slipped in behind them. The old shepherd and a stranger were warming their hands at the fire. The new man was obviously a seaman.

Looking about the cave he seemed a bit apprehensive, but not afraid. Then he was aware of the two armed men. He jerked and reached for a knife at his belt. But Kerr placed a reassuring hand on his shoulder. Although nervous, the stranger returned Kennedy's stare steadily.

'We were getting a bit worried, Angus. Who is this?'

'This gentleman is going to get us to Inverawe,' chuckled Kerr as if at some secret joke. 'And I would like you to remember your manners and stop pointing guns at one of my friends.'

'But who is he? I thought no-one else lived on this side of the island.'

'His first name is Ivan. His surname I can't pronounce. It is some queer foreign gibberish.'

Kennedy and Carson gawked at the seaman.

'A Russian!' choked the Scot.

'Aye, he is that. But he is still going to get us to Inverawe.'

12

'A goddamn Red!' bawled Carson. 'You must be crazy.'

The seaman frowned at the American's red-faced anger.

'It could be worse,' commented the shepherd dryly. 'He could be English!'

Kennedy felt bewildered as he fumbled in his pockets for cigarettes. He offered the packet to their unexpected visitor. Ivan drew one out with a sudden grin. His teeth were strong, even and unexpectedly a brilliant white.

'Now let's calm down and talk this over,' he said pointedly to Carson. 'Relax and take it easy.'

They sat round the fire. The Russian produced a bottle from under his thick jersey and passed it round with a rigid smile. The shepherd held his head back and the clear liquid gurgled over his throat. Handing the bottle to his fellow Scot, he grunted that it was a smooth drop of stuff.

Kennedy swilled over a generous measure and pushed the bottle towards Carson. The private investigator ignored the gesture.

'Come on. The bloke is trying to be nice and it is good booze. Don't be childish.' His voice was a bit thick.

'Aw, what the hell!' mumbled the big man and reached out. The level of alcohol fell alarmingly in the bottle as he held it to his lips. Suddenly he shuddered and his head dropped between his knees.

'Jesus Christ!' he croaked. His throat and stomach blazed with an incandescent fire. 'You guys said it was smooth. What the hell is it?' He glared at the stranger.

'Vodka. Good, Yank, eh?' said Ivan, laughter dancing in his small dark eyes.

'Yeah good, Ruskie. Anyone who can produce booze like that can't be all bad.'

'Now that the start of the Third World War has been postponed, you can put us in the picture, Angus,' smiled Kennedy.

For some years the Russian fishing-boats had been using some Scottish ports to take on water and stores. Ivan was the skipper of one of those boats.

The reporter smiled to himself as the American's eyes widened as he heard of the discreet landings at Kerr's place.

'Just after we arrived here I spotted a craft out there,' pointed the old man. 'I thought it might be Ivan here.'

When he had gone off, it had been to his home.

'We have a simple system of signals,' he went on. 'Ivan came in and I told him of our problem. He will help.'

Kennedy leaned forward with an excited smile on his lean face. 'Can you take us over to the mainland?'

The Russian shrugged and turned to his friend.

'The man has only a little of the English, but I have taught him some Gaelic. I will ask him.'

Kennedy ran his hand over his unshaven face and grimaced at Carson. A Gaelic speaking Russian fisherman. What next?

The two men talked softly in the musical tongue, heads close together. By the sound of it, Ivan had more than a little of the Gaelic. Finally Kerr slapped him on the shoulder and turned to the others.

The Russian could not do that. The Navy frigate was cruising in the narrows. He could not take the risk of being caught by the Royal Navy. He could not even take the chance of passing a message either to the warship or the mainland.

'Damn it! Why?' cried Kennedy.

'There are men in his ship who are not as friendly as Ivan here,' said Kerr. 'The craft has also excellent radar equipment.'

'A spy ship?'

'Something like that, but it fishes too. A bit of smuggling is one thing. But if Ivan was even suspected of what you suggest, then . . . '

'Home,' grunted the fisherman and ran a finger significantly over his throat.

But the shepherd said that Ivan would take them in his dinghy and land them near Inverawe. If he kept close to the shore he doubted if either the Russian or Navy radar would pick him up. As it was he was still risking his neck.

The stocky fisherman sat crosslegged drawing away contentedly at the cigarette.

The strain had gone from his weather-beaten face.

Kennedy looked quizzically into his eyes. 'Why?'

Ivan gave a slow shy smile and placed a hand on Kerr's shoulder. 'My friend,' he said slowly. He waved his arm in a gesture that took in the other two men. 'His friends — my friends.'

The journalist had caught the sombre expression that had crept over the American's face and guessed what he was thinking. This Russian was quite a guy!

'What about his crew?' asked Carson. 'Won't they suspect something when he is late getting back.'

'Ivan has enough whisky in his wee boat to start his own pub,' averred Kerr strongly. 'That will be more than enough to keep them happy.'

* * *

The boat was a little less than twenty feet long and powered by a large engine. The exhaust noise was deadened by an underwater exhaust and over the motor

196

was fitted a wooden box that reduced the clamour of the power unit.

Kennedy caught the American's intrigued gaze on it. 'I would imagine that Ivan and Angus don't want to advertise their modest import/export business.'

Carson grunted something like approval.

The early evening breeze had dropped as the fisherman took his craft out of the bay. The bow was high as they hurried along. The island was a black shadow against the night sky as they ploughed through the oily sea.

Once when sliding out of a swathe of mist, they saw a ship's lights well to the east. Ivan leaned on the tiller and turned back into the mist's cover and even nearer to the rocky shore.

'Boom, boom,' cried the fisherman. His arm bent at the elbow and punched at the air. The Navy was still about. There was little chance of being picked up by the frigate's radar, but Ivan was taking no chances.

The shapeless shadow that was the old shepherd straightened. 'Do you hear that?' They all listened intently, but could only hear the muffled beat of the engine at their feet. He thought there was a plane about but could not be sure.

Kennedy sat well forward of the others. He cradled the sub-machine-gun in his arms like a baby to protect it from flying spray. The salt water was clean and fresh on his filthy face. The steady motion of the boat over the swell and the regular rhythm of the engine had a soporific effect. He let his mind wander and found himself thinking of Isla Armstrong.

It was the first time since fleeing the town that he had a real opportunity of allowing her memory to fully occupy his mind. Back there on the island, except for the odd fleeting moment of concern, he had been too busy staying alive to think of much else.

But out here on the water surrounding Bargrennan, he could really relax and think of the dark-haired girl.

He smiled to himself. It was funny but he could not recall what she actually looked like. Small and pretty with guts — that was about all. His memory cells could only produce a vague picture of her as if seen through a wet window. But his senses could remember her. There was a femininity about the dark girl that disturbed him deeply. The pulse in his throat began to beat faster.

A harsh whisper dragged him reluctantly from his dreaming back to reality. The boat had slowed considerably and was nosing through another belt of mist.

Their swarthy helmsman waved a hand from left to right. 'In loch,' he grunted. How he was aware of his position was a mystery to the others. In slow time he steered up the narrow neck of water nearer and nearer to Inverawe and McRee. Like stepping through a door they were suddenly free of the clinging mist and in open water.

The town lights shone right ahead and across the loch the castle was also ablaze with light. Every window gleamed and torches flared on the battlements. The black mirror of the loch reflected the tinsel and spangle of it all. The strident shriek of bagpipes sounded through the still air.

'Something big is on there tonight,' muttered Carson. 'I wonder if we are invited?'

The Russian gave a low growl and held up a hand. He wheeled into a handy bank of mist and switched off. The boat rocked gently and they listened.

The heavy throb of another engine was now quite clear. It was coming closer. Carefully they prepared their weapons and tried to pierce the wreaths of vapour that whirled and circled about them. The fisherman produced a pistol from beneath his seat.

The tall bow of a large boat stabbed through the mist and slashed past only feet from their gunwhale. Ivan had just regained control of his bouncing, pitching craft when the stranger returned. Fortunately the searching eyes were above the protective white blanket.

Kennedy cursed to himself. It must be some kind of guard boat, cruising back and forth at the mouth of the loch. He waved desperately towards the shore at the town side. Ivan nodded and started up.

Only a slight jar intimated that they had arrived. Very properly the Russian shook hands all round as they stepped into the knee-deep water. Not a word was spoken. Voices carry too well over water at night.

The private detective from Las Vegas pushed his shoulder against the sharp bow and in seconds their strange ally was swallowed in the night. Only the half imagined sound of the engine showed that it had ever been — and then even that faded away.

Kennedy took in every shape and sound about him. It seemed clear. He waved an arm and they spread out, moving across the sand to the road. They dropped prostrate beside the black tarred ribbon.

Between them and the township was a small wood. The road passed through it.

'I bet there is a guard just where the road enters the trees,' he whispered. A bright stab of red light as a careless man felt in need of a cigarette confirmed his suspicions.

Carson wanted to slip forward and take

201

him. No — McRee must not suspect their presence in town. They would circle the wood. The manse would be their first stop. On the edge of Inverawe, it would be easy to reach without being spotted. The minister could brief them on the state of affairs in town.

Thirty minutes later — it seemed much longer — they slipped through a small gate in the high wall surrounding the 18th-century building.

The Reverend McLeod ushered them in quickly. Isla Armstrong was seated in the drawing-room. She gasped when she saw Kennedy's bloody, tattered appearance.

'I am not as bad as I look,' he said lightly. 'All I need is some soap and water.'

The practical girl pushed him into a chair and rushed from the room. Kerr followed her to get some food from the kitchen.

The American folded on to a couch. 'Sir, you must forgive me but I am finished. I have partaken of more exercise in the last twelve hours than I have in the last twelve years. Serves me right for joining these two mountain goats!'

He closed his eyes and was immediately asleep, but his hand still rested on the Colt stuck behind his belt.

The elderly minister turned on Kennedy. 'You are in great danger here,' he warned tersely. 'The Chief's men are everywhere. Isla has told me everything. McRee thinks I am rather an ineffectual old man but I will help you in any way I can.'

The girl returned with a basin of hot water and clean towels. As she bathed the dried blood and dirt from his face and hands and then redressed his wound, he brought her up to date on what he and the others had gone through.

He felt a perverted pleasure in watching her concern as he spoke of his flight and battles in the hills. Their eyes met and it was the man who turned away stirred by the raw emotion the girl displayed.

Her eyes glistened as she held back tears as he told her of John's death.

'You are an extremely lucky young man,' commented the minister in a remarkably steady voice. 'I cannot condone the killing that has gone on. All my life I have preached forgiveness but in McRee's case I find it difficult to do so. You had to kill or be killed but McRee is a murderer — a foul murderer. His soul belongs to Satan!'

Kennedy recalled the old woman's farewell. She had felt the same about the Chief's soul.

'That is why we are here, sir,' returned Kennedy firmly. 'If I can take him, then the others will be helpless. Without their leader they are nothing. And we can get word to the mainland and clean up this filthy business once and for all. I think I stand a chance of pulling it off. It is the last thing they would expect.'

'That's impossible now, David,' said Isla uneasily. 'His men are everywhere. His story is that there is a gang of deer-poachers from Glasgow in the hills, and that they have already taken a shot at some of his men.

'He persuaded all the townsfolk with boats to take them over to the castle harbour where they could be guarded.

Some of his men were in the hotel earlier and I overheard them say there is to be an important meeting in the castle tonight.'

The minister frowned and walked over to the fire where he stared into the dancing flames.

'The Chief of the Clan McRee a murderer!' he whispered. 'But why? He is rich and a much-respected man who has done a lot for the island. In God's name, why?'

Kennedy shrugged and grimaced as the antiseptic stung his injuries. 'I have an idea what is behind it all but no proof. That is another reason I want to get over to the castle tonight.

'If I am right, then it is much bigger than just murder on a lonely Scottish island!'

* * *

The tapping of her heels was loud as she strolled casually down the wooden pier. At the end Isla stared over at the brilliantly lit castle perched on its pinnacle like something out of a Walt Disney film.

The young man cradling a shotgun in his arms stepped forward from the shadow of the small office used by the harbour-master.

'It's a captivating spectacle, isn't it?' He had a soft and very correct voice.

She agreed. It must have been hundreds of years since there was a similar display.

He moved closer to the attractive girl. She was older than him but very beautiful. She was out late and there was a touch of concern in his tone.

'Should you not be indoors?'

Isla turned on him and replied testily, 'There is no law against going for a short walk, is there?'

The young man stammered an apology. 'I was just thinking of those hooligans from the city.'

The girl felt her initial, hidden fear fade and restrained a strong desire to giggle. The boy was only about twenty and clearly uncomfortable. It was absurd that she had to play the temptress and take his attention away from the loch.

She stepped nearer to him. Her breasts

brushed his chest and she raised her face. Her large dark eyes smiled intimately and he hurriedly took a pace backwards. This situation had not been included in the instruction he had received from McRee's older mercenaries.

'But I feel safe with you,' whispered Isla intently. 'What is your name?'

'Ian.' He shuffled a little.

She reached out and touched his arm softly. 'Ian, stand still. If you keep on moving away from me you will fall over the edge. You are not afraid of me, are you?'

Glancing over his shoulder he stiffened. 'Of course not, but I should not be speaking to you. I am supposed to be on guard.' There was a touch of bravado in his voice now.

Isla Armstrong was a normal woman and she was beginning to enjoy teasing the young man.

'Don't be silly. The Chief is over in the castle and we are here — alone. Who can see us?' Her slim fingers ran lightly over the barrel of the gun. 'Where are you from?'

Ian positively twitched. 'Argyll,' he got out. He gawked as the fingers wrapped round the barrel.

'The men in Argyll are so big,' sighed Isla and leaned towards him. A dazed expression spread across his face.

Only a few feet below the couple, Kennedy crouched on one of the thick teak beams. He had stripped to shirt and slacks and on his feet were an old pair of gym shoes that the Reverend McLeod had found in a cupboard. Tied round his waist in a sealed plastic bag was his pistol.

He grinned at Isla's performance. He had never imagined the girl had it in her. But she was fortunate in her victim. It could have been someone tougher and older.

He slid off the beam into the black water. Limpet shells tore at his hands. The icy water made him gasp. Using a smooth breaststroke, he headed out towards the shining stronghold.

Risking a swift glance, the girl imagined she saw his head glide away. Her heart missed a beat and she offered up a short prayer for his safety. But he still needed a few more minutes.

'Come over to the hotel, Ian, and have a drink with me.'

But he stuttered that he could not leave his post.

She slipped her arm through his. At least he could walk her to the end of the pier. She would like that.

Standing behind the glass door of the hotel's front entrance, Carson chuckled. 'She has done it. Davie boy is on his way.'

The American had wanted to accompany him, but honestly reckoned he did not have the ability to swim the loch. The road was busy and guarded and it seemed unlikely that they could have got through that way. So Kennedy was going in on his own and playing it by ear.

The reporter felt very exposed as he swam easily across the narrow neck of water. But he was sure that any guard would be unable to see the surface of the loch clearly from his high post on the walls because of the bright lights.

He had no plan of action and did not even know how he was going to gain entry, but he could not stay hidden and inactive. Gradually he closed on the cliffs.

Treading water, he looked up at the towering granite face with something like despair. He ran his hands along the base of it and found the stone polished smooth by the beating waves of a million storms.

He swam along the wall searching for a break. In anything like a sea, he would have been dashed to death in seconds.

Not a crack or ledge broke the symmetry of the rampart. Kennedy pulled himself along to a cave that he had noticed during the ferry crossing. It was not really a cave but a thin slender crack that gaped open like the jaws of a pike. It only stretched back a few feet. He reached up and ran his numbed fingers over the wall on one side. The very edge of the cave was fractured with tiny cracks, maybe just enough to give the minimum of toe and fingerholds. How far up would they go? It would also mean attempting to scale an overhang at the top.

His finger curled over the broken rock and he hauled himself from the water. The lights above assisted slightly, but he made the climb mainly by touch. The wet soles of the gym shoes proved treacherous. Slowly he dragged his dripping body upwards.

Gaining height the crack narrowed into a chimney. Levering his body into it, Kennedy braced a leg against each side and kept going up. His calf muscles cracked with strain and his wounded shoulder was acting up. Suddenly the chimney came to a point.

For a moment panic hit him hard. He was stuck. Far below the loch awaited his headlong plunge into its bosom. Fear fed him fresh energy.

He stretched a hand above him and ran it over the face. Grasping fingers found a slim crevice. Sliding a hand into it, he clenched his fist. Gradually he let himself slip out of the chimney until he was hanging from his clenched fist. Biting his lips against the agony tearing at his arm, he searched furiously for another hold.

His left foot settled on an inch-wide ledge and his terror escaped in a strangled gasp. His spare hand gripped a tussock of rough grass that somehow was securely rooted. Opening his fingers, he released his fist. Warm blood trickled down his forearm.

Sweating brow against the cold granite, he rested until his racing heart slowed to a steady beat. The cliff face was much more broken here. Frost and rain had worked on it. Grass and even the odd stunted rowan tree had found a home in minute scraps of wind-carried soil.

Progess was now swift and easy. A few feet higher and he scrambled on to a broad step where he collapsed. His breath came in great quick gulps. His whirling brain slowed down.

He had reached the castle wall and a fraction above his outstretched fingers was the dark outline of an arrow slit. There was no other seemingly available point of entry within reach.

Seven hundred years of attack from harsh winds had crumbled the mortar between the huge faced stones. It was finger-tip climbing again. It was a tight struggle to force his body through the narrow slit and most of his shirt did not make it. The rough stone slashed his chest.

A corridor within, damp and unlit, wound its way through the thick walls. It was no broader than his outstretched arms and pistol forward he crept along. The silence was heavy and pregnant with menace.

He reckoned it must have been a defensive position against attack from the sea. By the dust kicked up by his shoes, it was rarely used.

He stumbled over a step and his fingers found a stairway going up. Counting the steps he had reached twenty when a thin strip of light appeared level with his eyes. The bottom of a door. He opened it a fraction.

On the other side was a well-lit and thickly carpeted hall with two doors leading from it.

For the moment irresolute, he stood eyes flickering like those of a hunted animal. He believed he was on the third floor — but that did not help much. What door to take? The pistol was slippery in his hand and he rubbed it dry on the carpet. Taking a grip on his nerves, he swung the nearest door open.

It definitely belonged to a woman — or maybe a funny bloke. A shining white carpet covered the floor and modern white bedroom furniture softened the plain wooden panelling. White velvet curtains cut out the night. A huge Victorian four-poster covered in delicate white lace stood in the centre.

It was empty.

He caught a sight of himself in a mirror. A filthy, ragged, torn and bloody freak stared back. Tousled hair hung over a yellow and bruised face. The unshaven jaws emphasized his exhausted state. His shirt was in shreds. Fresh blood covered his shoulder.

Another door hung partly open — a bathroom. He went to find a towel. As he entered a heavy scent-bottle descended on his skull. But he did not really feel the crashing blow. He fell into a night that went on forever.

13

With awareness came pain. Daggers stabbed at his eyes and knives carved slashes across his skull. Slowly he began to orientate himself.

He forced his eyes open and found himself face down over a table. With an effort that brought a whimper, he levered himself upright and gaped incredulously about him.

It was the big main hall of the castle. Hundreds of candles guttered in holders on the walls and on the tables. Thirty-odd fierce-looking men were feasting. Modern weapons lay at their feet. Jugs of wine and beer were set at every elbow.

His head buzzed with the clamour of shouted conversations. A piper striding up and down at the far end added his contribution to the overpowering uproar.

He was seated at a small table at the head of the long room. It was set on a platform above the others. Food of all type was spread before him.

The Chief of the Clan McRee, resplendent in full Highland regalia, was on his left and in deep conversation with his neighbour — an immaculately dinner-suited Bernie McGuire!

McRee must have sensed that he had come to because he turned with a smile. 'You must have something to eat, my dear sir,' he cried and placed a goblet of red wine and platter of selected titbits of game before his prisoner.

Kennedy replied with a grunt and fell to. The wine helped soothe his thumping skull and he crammed meat into his mouth. Finally he leant back with a sigh of satisfaction.

For the first time in days Kennedy felt fully relaxed. What he had been afraid of had happened. The fear of being caught was gone and he was in McRee's hands. He did not have to think ahead as he had no future — but he was not dead yet. He was living from second to second. What happened now was all that mattered. Someone might make a mistake or relax and then he had to be ready to move.

McRee had finished his conversation with his fellow American and turned to his prisoner. The hawkish face was now set and grim, but there was a touch of triumph in the eyes. Malice was also there. He ground the point of a jewelled dirk into the table and twisted it.

'Tell me why I shouldn't have you killed?'

Kennedy felt as if the knife was turning in his guts. He shrugged and hid the fear in his eyes by sipping some wine. It was bitter to his tongue.

'Why didn't you kill me immediately I was caught? You did not have to invite me to dinner.' Somehow he felt that by showing courage he might win some time. A sign of weakness and he was finished.

He felt as if he was living a vivid dream. Alex's murder had started it all. At first he had been following up a good story. Now he knew that he wanted revenge. He wanted this man dead. The cruel glint in McRee's gaze was no fantasy and the iceberg in his stomach was no dream.

'Naturally I wanted to discover how much you knew,' replied the Chief.

Kennedy's face was a blank. He tapped the table with his fingers and pushed the glass away as if coming to a decision.

'You have been behind all the big bank and payroll raids that have been going on in this country for the last couple of years!'

His captor threw back his head and guffawed. His hand banged the table and he fought to control his laughter.

'Ridiculous, Kennedy! I expected better of you. How could I do that sort of thing from his remote little island?' Something like mischief shone in his sharp eyes.

'I know you killed Campbell, Houston and the other young copper. You would not have done that unless you were hiding something really important. But at first I couldn't work out what. Then it came to me on that first night on the run. From the hills I watched the fishing fleet out in the sound and it dawned on me. Every one of those robberies took place in a coastal town or city. Or one on a big river or estuary. Places where boats would not be out of place.

'That is why police roadblocks never

came up with anything. That is why the raiders vanished off the face of the earth. They escaped by sea!

'You used that big launch of yours or one of your own fishing-boats.

'And not one of your boys is a professional criminal. They are amateurs. No wonder the police were baffled.'

McRee slapped the table with both hands and a crystal glass fell over and smashed unnoticed.

'And what brought you to Bargrennan? What put you on to me?'

McGuire had stood up and had stepped behind the Chief's high-backed chair. There was an unnatural stiffness about the normally relaxed gambler.

Kennedy explained glibly that it had been a hunch. Houston had been unhappy about Campbell's death and it had also been after his visit here that he claimed to possess a lead on the raids. He hoped McRee would swallow it. He made no reference to the Club Scarlet and the photograph there.

He was rewarded with a slim smile from McGuire. The gambler now owed him but would he pay up? He would have to wait and see.

'And where are Carson and that damned old shepherd?' interposed his neighbour.

He was not sure. Still up in the hills somewhere, he imagined.

'A remarkable story from quite a remarkable man,' grunted McRee. 'Almost single-handed you fought against me — and did very well.'

'Not really. Most of your men are unused to handling firearms. Maybe they have shot a couple of birds now and then, but facing another man with a gun in his hands is something else. By the time I was twenty I had fought in two wars.'

'But what brought you from America to here?'

The Chief talked easily, almost proudly, about his past. 'I am a criminal,' he said frankly. 'I had a very nice operation going in Las Vegas when the law began to close in on me.'

Then out of the blue came word from Scotland that he was now Chief of the Clan McRee. It was his let-out. He got rid of all his interests in the States and came to Bargrennan.

At first he confined his aims to building up a front. He became a highly respected and distinguished figure on the Scottish scene. But all the time he was reviving the island's economy, McRee was planning.

'My first move was to bring over one of my best men,' he explained. 'A superb planner who was not even suspected by the police. I gave him a new identity and a new business.

'McGuire is a veritable master in his field. A brilliant planner and organizer. It was his idea to escape by sea. Who ever heard of roadblocks in the English Channel?'

And it had been his brainwave to recruit amateurs. Some were former mercenaries but most were youngsters teetering on the edge of crime. They were each specially trained for their future role.

Campbell had been caught nosing about the Tower and had to die.

'But why kill Houston?'

'He suspected one of my Glasgow contacts,' rasped McRee.

Kennedy leaned back in the chair and rested his head against the hard wood. The earlier pick me up of the wine had slipped away and all he wanted to do was sleep, but that was a luxury he could not afford. Sleep now and he would never wake up.

'What now?'

McRee's eyes flashed and his voice deepened. The dirk flew from his hand and slammed into the floor at the prisoner's feet where it stood quivering.

'This was to have been a final dinner. With you on the loose I was well aware that I could not hide the truth much longer. I could not keep the island cut off for much longer. The mainland authorities have already started asking questions. We were packing up and leaving at dawn. That boat of mine could take me anywhere in the world.

'Your capture has altered the picture drastically. I might be able to salvage all yet. That pompous Carson and old man will be no problem without you to back them.'

Little do you know them, thought

Kennedy. But he also realized there was a chance the man might just get away with it. There was no real proof against him. It was just their word against his. He did not even have to kill them. Even the explosion in the Tower could be explained. And who would doubt the word of the Chief of one of the oldest clans in Scotland? About his own future — or lack of it — he had no doubts at all.

'Later tonight you are going to die, Kennedy! I could have used you in my organization, but I have a feeling you are an honest man.' McRee made it sound like an insult.

He went to signal forward two brutal-looking men from the tables below, but McGuire held his arm.

'Leave him to me,' he offered.

'Right. Put him in the bottle dungeon. He will not escape from that.'

The dinner suited American drew a small flat pistol from a side pocket and waved the reporter to his feet. Reaching out his spare hand, he pulled a silver table-knife from inside the tattered shirt. Chagrin twisted Kennedy's face.

'You see, I always pick the best,' laughed McRee.

The torture chamber was empty and there was no sign of McKay. He was most probably at the bottom of the loch. Torment wrapped round him like a blanket and the screams of countless previous victims seemed to be trapped within the walls of stone. His skin shrank away from the touch of the damp air.

The man with the gun had an odd mien of uneasy apology about him.

Kennedy leaned against the wet rock. 'This madhouse doesn't seem your scene, McGuire. You are no killer.'

'That's damned right,' grumbled his captor tossing him a cigarette. 'I sometimes wonder why I got involved in the first place.'

The journalist lit his smoke from the proffered gold lighter. 'How did it come about?'

McGuire had ran one of McRee's casinos in Las Vegas. And he had a very lucrative sideline — planning robberies. His plans were good.

'You might not believe this but I am a

trained bank architect,' he confessed. 'And the killing did not seem so important over there. The cops have guns, the security men have guns — even housewives carry them in their shopping-baskets.'

Unhappily he flicked his half smoked cigarette into the well. His prisoner stood mute and still. There were times it paid to shut up and wait.

An angry scowl worked over the American's handsome face. 'But the killings over here were different. Unarmed men and women shot down in cold blood. I tried to plan in such a way that no-one would get it — but they always did.'

Kennedy knocked the ash carefully from the end of his cigarette and examined the red glow carefully. 'Why don't you split? I have friends over in town. You could hide out with them.'

McGuire let out a bitter laugh. 'You must be kidding. Cross that bastard and I'm dead.'

Kennedy swung away from the wall and stepped forward until the weapon was digging into his stomach. There was a cold anger and contempt in him for this man.

'You make me sick. Standing there claiming you don't like all the killing. Yet you fingered Alex Houston and got him gunned down in a filthy Glasgow street. You are not just a crook but yellow with it.'

The gun slashed alongside his ear and smashed him against the wall.

'That's a lie,' screamed McGuire. 'I had nothing to do with it. I told you the truth. He only wanted me to keep an eye open for hot money.'

Did they speak in his private room?

'Of course, cops about the place can give it a bad name,' answered the American with some of his old spirit.

It was after the detective had left that he had remembered the Bargrennan photograph. He didn't reckon Houston had noticed it but thought it better to take it down. After the fire he had found the writing-table drawer forced open and guessed what had happened.

'I didn't tell McRee about it. If he had found out that I had that picture on show he would have had my guts. He was always adamant that nothing connect us. That is why the only time I visited up here I stayed at the castle. No-one on the island met me. Thanks for shutting up about it.'

Kennedy thought for a moment. 'There is someone else in Glasgow then. Who is it?'

The gambler shook his head stubbornly. To reveal that would be signing his own death-warrant.

'No matter. I think I know who it is. Now you had better dump me in my cell.' Standing about was not going to get him out of this hole, but he would give McGuire a farewell to worry over.

'I will be waiting for you in hell, lad.'

What was that supposed to mean, insisted McGuire.

The Scot smirked. 'You are already as good as dead. Whether McRee likes it or not his organization is breaking up. Important people in Glasgow will look closely into my disappearance.

'Of course, he will try and cover up. And as his top planner, you will be first to go. You will be a dangerous embarrassment. You are dead, Bernie, but not quite buried yet.'

For a moment the man was shaken. He wiped the sweat from his face with a silk handkerchief, but he had not survived in the tough American rackets by wetting himself at the first sign of danger. His mind was already turning over ideas to get him out of this mess in one piece.

'Now if you turn away for a second I might be able to help you in your dilemma,' suggested Kennedy slyly.

'Jesus! You are a trier,' smiled McGuire sourly. 'You haven't a cat's chance in hell of getting out of this joint. You got in by a fluke. They believed that cliff was unclimbable.

'There are so many men out there you would have to walk on their heads to get to the gate. I'm real sorry, but there is nothing I can do for you. I am going to have enough trouble looking after number one.'

Reaching down, he raised a heavy round wooden trapdoor set in the stone floor. He waved his prisoner to the edge.

The reporter stared down into the bottle dungeon and his face must have betrayed some of his despair.

Escape-proof — a cell shaped like a bottle carved out of the rock. He eased himself into the neck and climbed down a rope ladder into its depths.

'I will leave the light on,' shouted McGuire framed in the hole.

Kennedy thought of Isla and his other friends waiting at the hotel. They had to get off the island somehow.

'Bernie, you will be lucky if you see tomorrow's sunset. How far can I trust you if I give you a chance of staying alive? A slim one — but still a chance. You are finished if you stay here.'

The slim man with the gun grinned. 'Any chance I will take. But you stay down the hole.'

Kennedy told him of his friends. They had to try and get to the mainland or hide out in the hills until help came from the mainland. 'And it will, believe me. Get to them. Your extra gun might make all the difference.'

McGuire's face appeared in the hole

for the last time. 'In return I will do you a favour.'

The man in the dungeon frowned.

'I will forget that dirk of McRee's that you plucked from the floor and stuck down your belt at the back!'

14

He examined his prison closely. The hatch was about 20 feet above his head. The diameter of the circular bottom about 12 feet. The cell had been chiselled out of solid rock. The whole thing was shaped like a good brandy-bottle.

The light was a heavy-duty fitment more suitable for a ship than a Scottish dungeon. He offered up a blessing that it was fairly dry. A rickety wooden table and straw mattress covered with a soiled brown blanket were the only furniture. Sitting on the edge of the table, he set his mind to thoughts of escape.

McRee alleged it was escape-proof. But the remembrance of what had happened to Houston, McKay and the little barman was encouragement enough to think of a way out.

It was a waste of time standing on the table — his fingers only grasped at empty air. Even if he smashed it and tore the blanket into strips, he could not make any sort of ladder that would be high enough. And the smooth walls would have defeated an Alpine climber. Then there was that overhang at the top.

The American had thrown down cigarettes and a book of matches before dropping the trapdoor. He lit one and lay back on the mattress. He stared up at the hatch that led to life and freedom.

He dearly wanted to sleep. If only to escape from the aches of his battered body. His nerve ends throbbed and jumped and he was exhausted both physically and mentally. But his tenacious spirit kept directing his daydreams towards a way out of this prison.

Bizarre concepts that resulted in escape waltzed back and forth through his mind. The light grey smoke twisted up through the neck to be trapped hovering beneath the hatch. Just like him.

Thank God McGuire had left the light on. Darkness would have been too much ... the light! He scrambled up and jumped to where it was fixed to the wall. It was a heavy brass and glass fitment and a thick lead wire ran from it up through the edge of the trapdoor. It was attached to the wall by strong steel staples sunk into wooden plugs. They were about two feet apart.

Dragging the table across, he clambered up on it and ran his fingers over the cable. Between the staples he could just slip his fingers behind the wire.

Here was the opportunity he was searching for. But there was still one problem — the overhang at the neck. He would be hanging by his fingers and would have to depend on the strength of his arms alone to climb the rest. In his condition that was out of the question. His gaze fell on the blanket.

Jumping down, he whipped out McRee's dirk. In five minutes he had an armful of blanket strips each about a yard long. Tying them in loops, he hung them about his neck.

Back on the table, he slipped one through the wire a few inches. Taking the other end he passed it through itself and pulled tight. A loop now hung from the cable. A few feet up, he repeated the action.

Kennedy put his foot in the first loop and reached up to grasp the thick wire. It accepted his weight. Now his other foot in a higher loop and pull up. Slip through another strand of blanket and make another loop. The electrician who had installed the light had done a good job. The plugs and staples held firmly.

The overhang proved nearly too much for him in his weakened state. His torn shoulder made him gasp. Vague ghost-like shapes floated in front of his eyes. Another loop. It was now proving awkward to get his feet into them.

'Just one more,' he bullied himself time and again. Then his bleeding knuckles struck the hard seasoned wood of the hatch.

'God, what if it is locked,' he groaned aloud. But it was not.

The damp stone flags were cold against his burning cheeks. His sight cleared and he ceased trembling. Now to find McRee. Holding the dirk point upwards, he climbed the stairs.

The main hall was empty and debris from the feast covered the tables. The candles were spitting like angry cats as one by one they spluttered out. The Chief's Hall on the next floor was also deserted. No sound filtered through the thick walls as he held his breath to listen.

He was not at all sure what he was going to do if and when he found McRee. His first instinct was to let daylight into him with his own dirk. But he doubted if he could kill the man in cold blood. Anyway he would be valuable as a hostage.

As usual you are playing it by ear, he thought glumly.

He hesitated outside the door to the Chief's private sitting-room. He could pick up nothing through the thick wood. The hinges turned smoothly and without sound. Blinking against the glare of the sudden brightness, he saw McRee — and Margaret Anderson!

They were at the window. McRee whirled, annoyance on his face. At the sight of his freed prisoner, he swore and leapt for his desk in a whirl of tartan.

Kennedy threw the knife desperately and missed. The Chief's fingers were just closing around the grip of an automatic when the blade flashed past his eyes and instinctively he jerked back.

The reporter dived across the desk and carried the kilted man to the ground. Snatching at his hair — he smashed his skull unceremoniously against the floor.

When a dazed and bemused McRee scrambled to his feet, he found a pistol lined up on his forehead.

'Over there next to the woman,' ordered Kennedy sharply.

McRee staggered to the couch.

Margaret was trembling and the blood had fled from her attractive face. A tremulous smile hovered about her full lips, but her eyes were blank. A red anorak and slacks complimented her almost Mediterranean looks. Her slim hands clasped a shoulder-bag tightly on her lap.

'How did you escape?' grated the Chief. Spittle ran down the side of his mouth. 'Who helped you? He will die.' Words tumbled wildly from his twisted mouth.

The man behind the gun smiled.

'Faraday helped me.'

'Faraday. Faraday. I know of no man of that name. He is not one of my men,' raged McRee. 'Who is he?'

'I believe he discovered electricity,' grinned Kennedy feeling a bit light-headed. He walked over to the open window and risked a glance out. A cool wind was nice and it was a dark night without stars.

He lifted himself up on to the broad ledge like a hopping bird. 'What are you doing with this scum, Margaret?'

Slim fingers fluttered nervously about her throat. Her breath was sucked in with soft sobs and moisture glistened at the corners of her eyes.

'They kidnapped me, David,' she faltered. 'I'm so frightened. Please help me get away.' The plea shook her voice and even her eyes held his. Her hands went out to him. 'I think they are going to kill me!'

The battered man scowled bitterly. There was a sickness in his stomach that made him gag.

'Good. That will save me the job!'

Her fingers unconsciously curled into claws and the scarlet nail-varnish made them appear as if they had just been dipped in fresh blood. Her body bent forward like a frightened, angry cat trapped in an alley.

'What do you mean, David?' she croaked. 'You were Alex's friend.'

He straightened up on the window-ledge. The room was silent except for the slapping of the sea against the cliff far below.

'You want help? After you helped send Alex to his death. You — his fiancée. But then all along you didn't give a damn about him. You used the man. You were in with this bastard here and fed him information only a senior police officer would know. How did you get that information out of Alex? Show a future wife's interest in his work or something like that?'

His stomach heaved again as he thought of her betrayal. He had liked the girl himself and could easily have fallen for her. He wanted to throw up.

He did not know all the details and

much of it was guesswork, but it all added up. The big detective had discovered a link between Campbell's death, Bargrennan, Margaret and the Club Scarlet.

'Just how he did this I doubt if we will ever know. But if a hack writer like me could do it, a skilled copper would find it easy. On the night Alex died, he called on you. He most probably told you of how well he was doing on the case. I bet that frightened you, Margaret.

'So you gave him a drink and lit a cigarette for him with a match from one of the specially made Club Scarlet books. It would give you time to think. Alex recognized it for what it was. I am sure he had been watching the club for some time. But he had never taken you there. A big plain copper with a beautiful girlfriend. Had you gone there with someone else? The thought would torture him. Were you tied up with the raids? Enough to drive any man mad.

'So he phoned me. Didn't I get you two together? He wanted to ask me some questions. I didn't know it then but they were about you. And you had him shot down.'

The girl sneered and it made her ugly. 'Rubbish! Alex took me there only the other week.'

'Stop lying in your teeth. McGuire told me Alex had never been to the place socially.'

Her eyes had become pinpoints of diamond-tipped hate. A flicker of tension worked at the corner of her mouth and her lips pressed together in a thin line like those of a spinster schoolteacher about to take out her hang-ups on the backside of a scared schoolboy.

'You are McRee's contact in the city. He was on to you and had to die. He must have said he was going to have a word with me. That's why you phoned the office and found out where we were meeting.'

It was all circumstantial with loose ends waving about all over the place. It would never stand up in court, but it added up.

While he was speaking, she had managed to get a hold on her emotions. Only anger showed now. An anger held under tight control. Her blazing eyes showed contempt for his theories.

'But you never told me where you were meeting for a drink,' she said softly but with menace.

'I didn't have to. I said I was going to police headquarters. Your murderer picked me up there and I led him to the pub.'

Suddenly Kennedy was sick of the whole business. He just wanted to get it over and done with. He wanted out of the castle and back with the lovely girl across the loch.

'You haven't got one real fact to support your foul story,' cried Margaret. Her eyes softened. 'What has happened to you here has tried you terribly. I can't blame you for suspecting everyone, but you are wrong about me. Let me help you escape.'

The hand gripping a heavy pistol was resting on the ledge beside his hip. The wrist moved a fraction and the barrel lined up on her beautiful face. Other than that small but threatening movement, he ignored her words and went on as if she had never spoken.

'When I came round to console you, I helped myself to a match from that same little book. It wasn't until later I found out what it was. And that first made me suspicious of you, lass. Then all those attacks on me. Only you were aware of my movements. I had to get the chop as well.

'By the way, Alex never did get a chance to tell me anything. Not in a way I understood anyway. As he was dying he urged me to 'get Margaret'. I thought at the time he wanted you by his side. Later I realized what he really meant. He wanted me to get you and put you away for a long time — in jail!'

Fires blazed in her eyes and ignoring the weapon she went to leap at him, but McRee pulled her back. Kennedy wondered for a second if he would have pulled the trigger.

'Sit still,' ordered McRee. 'What are your plans now, Kennedy?'

'You are going to take me to the radio room. There I am going to contact the authorities or that frigate out there and get the police in. Now on your feet and let's move.'

Margaret bent forward to stand up

from the low couch and pulled a small pistol from her bag. A snap shot peppered him with splinters of stone. The big automatic jumped in his fist. An ugly red flower burst into bloom on her forehead and she slammed back over the couch. Her dead eyes still held her final thoughts of hatred and death.

He tried to swing the pistol on to McRee but it was too late. A hastily flung bottle thumped against his wounded shoulder and was enough to knock him back. A laugh followed him as he tumbled out of the open window. His fingers scrabbled at the smooth stonework. A scream was forced from his lungs as he plunged into space.

He turned over and over, arms and legs flailing. The sound of air rushing past his ears was deafening. Hitting the water was like crashing into a brick wall. The air was punched from his chest.

Down and down he went until his feet sank into soft mud. Seaweed wrapped round his legs and childhood nightmares flooded his mind. Frantically he pulled upwards. His left arm was useless and his lungs began to burn and lights flashed on and off inside his skull.

With no warning his head and shoulders jumped clear of the surface. He floated on his back and dragged in air. High above were the lighted windows of the fortress. McRee would send round a boat to check. He had to get away. He clawed at the water with his right hand. He found that he could move his left arm, but there was little strength in it. His legs kicked wearily. A numbness was creeping over his body and bringing with it oblivion.

Drowning was supposed to be an easy way to go, but he was not finding that. Salt water filled his mouth and he went under. Legs thrashing feebly, he managed to lift his head clear again. Senses sliding away and bolts of white lightning filling his skull, his vitality finally failed. What the hell, he thought, and without remorse or fear slid beneath the bouncing waves.

The bite of whisky on his throat sent him into a fit of violent coughing and, rolling over on his side, he was terribly ill. His stomach emptied itself of seawater and his last meal. He opened his eyes and saw that he had just been sick over the carpet in Isla Armstrong's office.

'Thank God! I didn't want to give you the kiss of life. That would have been too much.' Carson's booming voice sounded wonderful.

Strong hands lifted him and placed him on a chair. Behind Carson grinned McGuire.

'Goddamn it, Kennedy, you did it! How the hell did you get out of that dungeon and then the castle?'

His throat was tender, but he explained quickly. 'How did I get here? The last thing I remember is passing out in the loch.'

McGuire had slipped into the hotel a couple of hours earlier and told them of his capture. They were at their wit's end to know what to do when Isla remembered there was a boat in the hotel garage that had been missed by McRee's men.

The two Americans had managed to get it to the pier and launch it. They had heard him splashing about and McGuire had grabbed his hair as he went under.

'But what about the boy guarding the pier?'

'He'll never be a man,' growled the big private investigator gruffly. The good-natured face was stern and hard.

The old shepherd and Isla were out collecting some local men who could be trusted and were bringing them to the hotel.

While the detective had been talking McGuire had cut off the Scot's rag of a shirt. The shoulder wound had burst open again. He cleaned and dressed it with bandages from the hotel's first-aid cabinet. His fingers were deft and gentle.

'That will do for now, but get a doc to see to it real soon.'

'Where did you pick that up?'

'Courtesy of the US Army in Korea. The Army decided that with my professional experience of gunshot wounds I would make a great medic.'

★   ★   ★

His back was against the bar and his knees trembled with strain. But he was

246

afraid to sit down — he might never get up again. His eyelids seemed to be rubbing on grit.

He examined the men before him. About half a dozen were gathered in the room. They were all mature — between forty and sixty. They sat nervously at the small tables. By their dress, they ranged from farmers to professional types. One deep-chested chap with a rough-hewn face had to be Murphy, the coalman.

Kennedy started to speak and even to his own ears the story sounded fantastic. Their expressions ranged from humour to anger. He was not getting through to them. They did not believe him — and he could not blame them.

'Well that's it. A lot of good men have died because of McRee and I want to get him, but I need your help. He knows I might still be alive and he will also know now that McGuire has scarpered. It is my opinion that he will wrap up his organization here and get out.

'I want your help to stop that. Without it there is a very good chance that he will just vanish. I am sure he will have escape plans laid ready for something just like this.'

A thin man with the grey complexion of his profession — he was a solicitor — jumped up. 'I have never heard such an insane tale in my life. Roderick McRee arrived on this island and from an economic disaster turned it into a place with a future. Every man in this room admires and respects him. Yet you are telling us he is a murderer! You must be mad.'

'And where do you think he got that money for these improvements?' snarled Kennedy. 'By killing helpless men and women. McGuire, you tell them.'

The gambler made a complete break of his association with the Chief of Clan McRee. He made no excuses for himself but just kept to the facts.

But Kennedy could see that he was not getting through to them either. This was Bargrennan. Murder and robbery — they found it just too fantastic. Even parking and speeding offences were unknown on the island.

Another man interrupted to state that he agreed with the solicitor. But even if there was something in their mad story, they should leave it to the police.

The sunken green eyes in Kennedy's ravaged face despaired. They would never accept his account. Kerr they hardly knew — he was practically a hermit. And the two Americans were strangers.

The solicitor — his name was Fraser — asked Isla if she had actually seen any of the killings or had any proof against the Chief. She shook her head silently.

'There you are,' cried Fraser to the others. 'I am going home and would advise you to do the same. I will get in touch with the police tomorrow and get this thing sorted out.'

There was a cough at the back of the room and the Reverend McLeod threaded his way through the tables. There was a blistering fury in his normally soft eyes.

'Mr Kennedy, would you and your friends wait outside for a moment? I would like to talk to my parishioners in private.' There was steel in the old man's tone.

A quarter of an hour later he called

them back in. The bar was empty. Kennedy's shoulders slumped. They had all gone home.

'Do not look so downhearted,' declared the minister. 'Aye, they have all gone home, but they will be back in five minutes — with guns!'

Their weapons ranged from ancient shotguns to expensive sporting rifles. But he noticed they were all well-cared-for and handled with accustomed ease and long familiarity.

He remembered that practically all of these ordinary men — if not all — would have served in the Army. They would have fought in France, Korea, Malaya or Egypt. Each was a trained soldier. And fighting was like riding a bike — it was something you never forget.

'I would like to know how Mr McLeod changed your minds?'

Fraser allowed himself a thin smile. 'You could say we are more afraid of our minister than we are of the Chief of Clan McRee. And he convinced us you were telling the truth and needed help — our help. So here we are.'

A wiry fisherman of about sixty pushed his way to the front. 'I'm still a bit worried about these modern automatic weapons they have.' There was a low growl of agreement.

'What regiment were you in?' snapped Kennedy.

'The Seaforth Highlanders in the last war.'

'And what was the German like as a fighter?'

'Bloody good! But we were better.'

'That's my point,' impressed the reporter. 'McRee has a few mercenaries, but they have only fought untrained blacks. The majority are youngsters in their twenties who have never been shot at. They think fighting is what they see on television. After the show is over, the dead get up and walk away. Try and recall what it was like the first time a bullet shot past your ear. I can — and I was scared stiff.

'Letting you loose over there is like turning loose a pack of wolves in a flock of sheep.'

Fraser grinned again. 'You can depend on us, Kennedy. The minister has convinced us that McRee is a killer and that we can expect no help from the mainland. Well this is our island and we can clean up our own mess.

'But what I wouldn't give for a nice tank. I was in tanks in North Africa and France.' There was more than a touch of pride in his voice.

Kennedy found it difficult to imagine this typical dried-up country lawyer thundering over the desert sands and taking on Rommel's Panzers.

'It is funny you say that, because I have been thinking . . . '

15

Kennedy had just completed briefing the Inverawe men on his plan for the attack on the castle when McGuire and Murphy returned. The American's dinner suit and silk shirt would never be the same again. The black bow tie hung loose. He reminded the reporter of a young Bogart.

'It's round the back,' rumbled the coalman. 'We did what you wanted.'

The reporter signalled the solicitor to come outside. He wanted a tank . . . there it was.

'But that's only Murphy's old coal lorry.'

'Take a closer look and remember the lads over there are only armed with rifles and sub-machine-guns.'

Fraser walked round the vehicles. Behind the steel sides of the body was a line of 1 cwt bags of coal. The steel would not stop a modern high-powered bullet, but the coal would. Another two were lashed in front of the bonnet to protect the engine. One was perched on the passenger seat and the windscreen was knocked out.

'When the driver is in position we will place another heavy steel plate between him and the door,' explained the gambler. 'Except for his head, he should be pretty well covered. What do you think?'

Fraser was concerned about the tyres.

'If they are as inexperienced as we think,' grated McGuire, 'they will blaze away at the bodywork and forget them.'

The little lawyer walked around it again. There was a spring in his step that had not been there before. 'Lash some empty coal-sacks on top of the bonnet. I only need a couple of inches to see over and they should stop small-arms fire.'

'You only need a couple of inches?' asked McGuire.

'Aye. I am going to drive this beast. I doubt if it would have frightened one of the Panzer laddies in a bloody great Tiger, but it might just do the job here.'

Kennedy felt a sudden stab of doubt. The little solicitor seemed so resolute and cheerful. Was he right in dragging them into this?

Fraser caught his frown. 'Don't worry about us. We deal with our own problems in Bargrennan and we will muck out our own byre!'

Carson appeared carrying a crate of bottles which he placed in the rear of the makeshift tank. 'Molotov cocktails for the use of.'

Kennedy and Carson had been given deer rifles by the Inverawe men. The other American preferred his small lethal pistol.

Finally everything was ready and he called the men about him. 'Now remember Carson, McGuire, Kerr and myself will handle the castle end. All you have to do is to put the boat out of action and destroy or disable any planes at the airfield.

'Don't get involved in the castle fight. If it looks as if it is going badly for us don't try and help. Get out of sight and make your own way back to your homes.

'I don't want any of you killed.'

He hauled himself into the back of the

lorry and drew a lean hill farmer down beside him. He was thin, almost haggard, but his eyes were kestrel-keen.

'Fraser tells me you are good with that rifle.'

'I hit what I fire at.' The man was not boasting.

'Great. I would like you to take up position on that hill behind the castle. But lie quiet until you see we are in trouble. The range is about 400 yards and you will have a clear view of the courtyard and main entrance.

'Think you can do that?'

'Aye' was the laconic reply. Hillmen are not given to much talking.

Kennedy turned and banged on top of the driver's cab with his fist. It was time. At his feet were some ropes and cans that sloshed when moved.

'Still want dealt in, Bernie?' he muttered to a dark shadow on the other side. 'You needn't. You have already carried out your part of the bargain.'

The gambler shrugged. 'I'm with you. That bastard made me dance like a puppet. I am going to enjoy this.'

The reporter rubbed some coal dust on his face and the others followed suit. Sweat trickled down making white streaks like war paint on their taut features.

The lorry jerked and jumped out on to the shore road. Fraser seemed to be having some trouble finding the gears.

'What the hell am I doing here?' grumbled big Murphy.

'If you want out I quite understand,' muttered Kennedy.

'Och, it is not the fight that worries me, Mr Kennedy,' said the big man in a shocked tone. 'It's that damned lawyer behind the wheel of my lorry.'

'So what. He drove a tank in the war.'

'Aye, maybe he did that, but Charlie Fraser can't drive a car!'

Muffled laughter ran round the vehicle and Kennedy winced — now they tell him.

But the North African veteran kept the lorry on the road and raced along at a fair lick. There was still no hint of dawn, but the odd early-rising bird could be heard announcing the arrival of a new day. Kennedy wondered if it would be his last.

His mind turned to Isla as she was when he left the hotel. With her short ruffled hair and large sad eyes, she reminded him of a lost waif.

'Do you have to do this, David? You are in no fit state to fight. You should be in hospital.' Her voice had been like the delicate rustling of crisp autumn leaves in an evening wind.

'I have to stop McRee. There is no way of getting out of it. It is as if my whole life was leading up to this point. In a way I'm trapped. These men do not have to get involved, but they are willing to have a go. I must do it.'

Her face had been controlled and calm. Only her eyes betrayed the torment being held in tight rein. Standing on her toes, she kissed him lightly. Her lips had been as cold as a February frost.

A nudge from Carson brought him back to the present. They were coming up to the bridge over the small river at the head of the loch. Four men stepped into the approaching headlights with shotguns held high over their chests.

The reporter and detective stood side

by side. Their weapons rested on the roof of the cab. The quartet waved the lorry down. Their expressions showed puzzlement. But that was replaced with alarm as Charlie Fraser paid no attention to their signals. One fired a warning shot over the vehicle.

'Now,' screamed Kennedy. The two men slammed shots into the tight group. One gunman was lifted by the blast of fire and tossed over the parapet into the river. Another gripped his stomach with both hands and fell into a ditch. The remaining two scuttled madly into the trees.

The lorry hustled on and they dropped behind the protective bags. Jagged edges of coal jabbed unheeded into their ribs. A sprinkling of shots from the beach rattled against the steel sides. They banged and clattered, but did not pierce the rampart. Careful fire was returned at the tell-tale flashes of light. A high scream cut its way through the howl of the motor. Carson cursed and ducked too late as a bullet slit the top of an ear.

'Here's the castle,' shouted Kennedy. 'Forget the beach.'

The headlights bounced off the curtain wall and heads could be seen along the top. The islanders directed their spleen up at them. The Chief's men lost all interest in the view as a barrage of fire rippled along the wall like a lethal tidal wave.

The gatehouse loomed up and Fraser braked. The heavy gates were shut and secured. Three men jumped out from behind a buttress with machine-guns at their hips. They poured a continuous fire into the lorry. The racket was thunderclap-loud. The attackers were pinned down by the hail of bullets.

Unnoticed Kerr slid over the tailboard and crawled under the vehicle until he could see three pairs of legs standing astride. His shotgun barked twice and ripped the limbs to shreds. He snatched up the weapons and pouches of spare magazines from the moaning bleeding figures and threw them up to Kennedy and Carson who dropped their rifles.

Murphy swung an open gallon can of petrol through a first-floor window of the gatehouse, and then another. A fisherman tossed a bundle of burning rags after them. For a split second there was an empty silence and then a whoof of flame spewed out of the shattered opening.

The lorry shuddered into motion and the coalman fell back into Kennedy's arms. 'Now you see why Charlie could never pass his driving test!' he yelled.

The sharpshooting farmer had vanished. Sometime during the little battle he had vaulted nimbly over the side and ran for the hillside. He was now sheltering behind a rock looking down into the courtyard.

He watched as the lorry lurched to a corner of the high wall. While the others supplied covering fire, Kennedy swung a rope round his head. There was a small three-pronged anchor lashed to the end of it. It sailed up and over the wall. Pulled tight, it was a simple but efficient grapnel.

While the Bargrennan men sprayed the area with bullets to dissuade onlookers, the two Americans scrambled up to the top. Kennedy cursed as he found that with his injured shoulder he could not manage the couple of pulls required. But the old shepherd spotted his difficulty and with a heave tossed him over a shoulder. He snatched at the rope and pulled them both up in a remarkable feat of strength.

The others had made the corner tower in safety. Random shots were coming from the castle and the garden. The Scots scampered for the questionable safety of the small building.

The reporter flinched as lead licked at his clothing. And dived flat as Carson stepped out of the tower door ahead. Snarling, the big man lashed half a magazine down the sentry walk. The firing ceased. Kennedy and Kerr half crawled and squirmed to shelter.

The sniper on the hill watched as the lorry moved jerkily along the road. His sharp eyes picked out two of his friends from the village heading for the harbour.

The tower was an excellent defensive position — as it had been designed for hundreds of years before. The walls were four feet thick with two doors leading out on to the wall. Arrow slits overlooked the road and the courtyard. A rough wooden stair rose to the roof where there was a low parapet. Another went down to a heavy door that opened out on to the courtyard.

The gatehouse was well and truly ablaze with flames spurting from every window. The inferno lit up the whole front of the castle. Trees and bushes stood out in the red light. The firing died away and there was no-one in sight.

'Keep a watch on the castle main door,' advised McGuire tersely. 'And that other one on to the wall. They'll try and get out more men.'

A figure jumped up from behind a bush and scurried over the grass. A single shot from Carson brought him down. He tried to rise but another shot drove him forward on to his face. This time he was still. A widening pool of blood spread out from him.

A sudden fury of lead splattered about them. They returned careful bursts. Five kilted men burst through a hedge and charged the tower yelling insanely. The combined fire of the defenders zeroed in on them in a fatal cone. Caught in the open, two were immediately blasted into eternity. They crashed down legs and arms askew. The remainder fled for cover.

A flurry of fire spewed from the castle windows. It was more of a nuisance than a danger. As they watched the main door opened a fraction and the tall figure of McRee hurtled out and down the stairs to fade into the shadows. He was tracked by a trail of bullets from the tower but made it unscathed.

'At least he has got guts,' commented Carson softly.

The Chief's shouts were clear as he took control. Up till now the resistance had been haphazard. The hit-or-miss shooting ceased. They could expect more dangerous and intelligent fighting from now on.

He seemed to be organizing his men in the furthest and darkest corner of the yard. The rising and falling flames from the blaze created a polka of fast moving shadows below them.

A shrill shout heralded a hail of fire. The bullets were directed at the arrow slits and doors. Some found their way in and rebounded from wall to wall. The quartet flung themselves flat. Loud cries could be heard above the hammering.

'They are coming again!' screamed Kennedy and ignoring the fire reached a slit just in time to see a line of men running through the trees and bushes. The wind of slugs made him flinch as he brought his sub-machine-gun up. Something burned along a cheek. The yelling mob was only yards away. Then a hard shoulder bounced him aside.

The bulky figure of the shepherd filled the slit. His shotgun was held hard into his shoulder. There were puffs of cloth as bullets slammed into him. But with a roar, the first barrel discharged its lethal dose. The second blasted like an echo. The line was blown apart.

Like a tall pine being felled Kerr toppled back. McGuire dragged him to the side and ripped his shirt open.

'Has he bought it?' swallowed Kennedy.

'No, but he should have,' rasped the slim gambler, his fingers busy. 'He is bleeding like a stuck pig.'

A white light suddenly bathed the castle to be followed by a deep explosion and the floor shuddered. A bright glow appeared in the vicinity of the airstrip. Firing died away and McRee's men stared about them in dismay.

Charlie Fraser had made the airstrip and was doing what he had been trained to do four decades ago. And he had not forgotten any of his old skill.

They had a few moments respite as McRee reorganized his tactics. More men appeared at the windows and on the high battlements. Others perched on the wall opposite. Careful aimed fire smashed at every opening about them. Carson tumbled back. There was a cruel red streak across his forehead. They were well and truly pinned down.

Concealed in the anonymity of the darkness on the hillside, the farmer realized that now was his time to act. He carefully gave his fine rifle a final check. His own black faced sheep stood silently about him unaware of the drama enfolding below.

He lined his sights up on a point on the battlements where a twinkling flash appeared regularly. There it was again. No hurry now — take first pressure. Squeeze gently. There was a satisfying thump on his shoulder. A distant figure jerked upright and fell forward into space. It turned over and over in slow motion to the stones below.

Now that window on the far left. He could not see the result of his effort this time. But he knew that a gunman was either dead or had just received a bloody great fright. He would not be too keen to stick his head up again.

Regularly working the bolt, he pumped shot after shot at the castle. A man tumbled from an embrasure and was dashed on the stairs at the main door. He lay splayed and broken.

That Glasgow man had been right. This lot were a crowd of amateurs. If they had been Jerries or Japs, they would have spotted him after the second shot and he would have had to hightail it.

The superb marksmanship paid dividends. Fire fell away. Carson shuffled over to a slit. 'That sodbuster is picking them off like clay pipes!'

He lifted his weapon but was too late to

stop McRee racing back into the main building.

Kennedy shut his eyes and leaned against the cool stone wall for a moment. When he opened them the gambler was watching him seriously.

'Something tells me you are going to do something damned stupid, Kennedy.'

A bitter smile twisted the newspaperman's mouth. Red lights danced before his eyes. He just had enough strength left for one last effort.

'Give me covering fire,' he demanded harshly. 'I am going to try and get McRee. If I fail, hang on here until daylight. That bloody fire is sure to bring the frigate in to investigate. Anyway I have a feeling that McRee is about to make a run for it. Even he must realize it is all over here.'

Bent double he stepped out on to the wall. The castle looked an eternity away along the sentry walk. He scrambled over the flagstones and reached the end unnoticed. The door was ajar and a moaning figure was curled up behind it. He ran his hand over the wounded man and found a pistol.

'Don't shoot. It's me, McGuire.' The hoarse whisper made him wheel. 'I had to follow you. Kerr came round just as you left. He insisted I came with you. He is propped up against the door with that shotgun of his.

'The firing has died away out there. That sniper is keeping their heads down and I think some of them have had enough. I will watch your back.'

Kennedy was too tired to argue. At something between a walk and a trot they headed for the main hall. Only a few candles shed any light in the high vaulted chamber. Tables and chairs lay overturned. A broad ledge ran round the hall just under the high windows and embrasures. Five men stood firing down through them intermittently. They did not seem very keen at exposing themselves.

Blue snow clouds of gunsmoke swirled about. One of the men suddenly straightened right up on his toes as if reaching for the ceiling and fell back. His skull crunched on the floor ten feet below with the sound of a hammer hitting a ripe melon.

Kennedy pointed with his sub-machine-gun to the corner stairway and they dashed for it. The scene was much the same in the Chief's Hall and they slid behind some drapes.

McRee stood at the fire surrounded by his lieutenants. He tried to get a clear aim at him but failed.

The tall man was haranguing his followers with a bitter tongue. They shuffled their feet, sheepish and uneasy. They could not meet his blazing eyes.

'Only four and you cannot take them,' he roared. 'You are cowards. Our operations here are finished, but before we have any chance of escape those men must be wiped out. My plane is destroyed and that only leaves the boat. Now get out of here and kill them. Swamp that tower with men if need be, but kill Kennedy and his friends. I want them dead.'

The listening Scot noticed that McRee had slipped back into his normal American accent. He must have been nervous. For a moment Kennedy thought of just letting loose on the group, but there was no guarantee he would hit the man he wanted so badly. And an even chance that he and McGuire would get it. He decided he was not cast in the hero mould.

The Chief growled a few more instructions and then stepped through the door that led up to his private room. His lieutenants ran for the courtyard.

'Right let's go get the bastard,' snarled McGuire.

Keeping close to the wall, they sidled round to the door. As Kennedy reached forward to push it open, the gambler's hand hit him between the shoulder-blades. He fell to his knees and a burst of automatic fire cut along the stonework where his chest had been. Stone splinters slashed his skull and he swivelled to see that one of them had turned back. His gun was coming up again.

Desperately Kennedy sent off a single shot. The man crashed against the wall, fell sideways and lay silent.

But McGuire was sitting with both

hands pressed against his chest. A pool of blood was forming on his lap. There was a sort of astonishment in his eyes.

'Well I did promise to watch your back,' he sighed. 'I'm shot to hell inside. Can't feel a thing — so it must be bad.'

Kennedy went to drag him inside the door, but the wounded man shook his head wearily. 'No. I'd fall apart. Give me my gun and get to hell out of here.'

His pistol had been shattered by a bullet. Kennedy placed his sub-machine-gun beside the American.

'Jesus! If the boys back home could only see me now.' The pain was beginning and the words came hard but he still tried to grin. 'We have made the St Valentine's Day Massacre look like a Sunday school picnic. Now beat it. No-one will follow you while I am here.'

Kennedy could find nothing to say. He just nodded and touched McGuire's shoulder lightly.

He locked the door behind him with a large iron key. Through the thick oak he heard the faint sound of conflict. The American was not going out like a cornered rat but like a brave fighting man.

McRee was at his desk. Hate and anger had changed his face into a caricature in which his evil was emphasized. Shock and malice fought for the possession of his twisted features. He dropped a briefcase into which he had been stuffing papers.

The wounded man's pistol was steady in Kennedy's right hand. His left arm had finally packed up and hung uselessly at his side.

'Move and I will blast that fancy silver belt buckle right through your spine.'

McRee shook his head. 'Put that gun down and I might allow you to live. My men are at this moment finishing off your friends. You are on your own.'

The journalist imagined there was a note of desperation and even of fear in his voice. He backed to the door and locked it. He flicked the key out of the open window.

The Chief spoke again. 'Listen, man. Give me an hour and I will make you a rich man. Enough money to last you the rest of your life. To buy good living and beautiful women. Just let me get to my boat.'

Kennedy's finger tightened on the trigger and his opponent's eyes opened wide. 'No. I am not going to kill you — although you deserve to die. Your men are beginning to crack and some of my chaps have your damned boat. You are all washed up.

'So just shut up and sit down. That frigate will come in soon to help fight that fire at the gatehouse. The Navy likes to do little favours like that. And you and I will go to meet them.'

The tall kilted man stared at the gun for a long, long moment and then hauled himself erect as some of the old spirit worked back into his nerves.

'You are a fool. You will always be a nobody. Real success will always evade you because you are soft inside. I would have pulled that trigger a long time ago. Now I am different. I would sacrifice anything or anyone to achieve my final aim.'

He settled down on the chair behind the desk and seemed to slump in sudden despair. Then he exploded. His right hand flashed up clutching a skean dhu — the small knife every Highlander carries in the top of his stocking. It streaked across the room.

Kennedy threw himself to the side and fired, but knew he had missed.

McRee vaulted the desk and snatched a claymore from a display above the fireplace. Whirling the heavy sword above his head, he charged down on death. Kennedy took a split second to aim on the broad chest before firing. There was only a click — the weapon was empty! In his fatigue he had forgotten to check its load.

A fierce cry of triumph burst from the Chief and he lunged with the deadly Highland clansman's blade. The crouching man slapped it aside with the pistol and then threw it into the snarling face. Blood spurted over the glaring eyes.

Kennedy jumped to the wall and snatched the first weapon from the display that came to hand — a small battle-axe. He recalled that this had been Robert the Bruce's favourite weapon for close combat. Luckily for him little skill was required in its use.

Swinging the axe in a figure of eight, he faced McRee. The steel smashed against the sword blade and the Chief fell back. Suddenly he broke off the fight and jumped through another door in the corner of the room. The reporter scampered after him up a short flight of stairs to the flat roof of the fortress.

The Chief's flight had been deliberate, not cowardice. Here he had the advantage of space. Lightly he danced around Kennedy. Superbly fit, he soon began to wear his man down.

The axe became heavier and heavier. The strain of wielding it began to tell.

The blazing torches lent a mystic quality to their duel. A number of the Chief's men stopped firing at the tower below and turned to witness the combat that swayed back and forth across the roof.

McRee waved them back. 'This man is mine!'

The eastern horizon was golden as the sun climbed to reach it, but Kennedy could not admire the beauty of the dawn that most likely would be his last. He stopped the figure of eight and conserved his waning strength by attempting just to parry the lunging and swinging strokes of the claymore. His eyesight was hazy as he followed the glistening point.

McRee stepped back and let the sword point drop. His breathing was slow and easy. 'It won't be long now. I will spit you like corn on the cob.'

Again he danced into the attack. A badly parried stroke sliced the useless left arm. Fire burned up to his brain. McRee laughed and lunged again. The gleaming blade slid along the axe and buried itself in the Scot's forearm. His fingers opened and the axe dropped with a dull thud. He screamed as the point was withdrawn.

Whimpering in agony, he turned and scurried to the furthest corner of the roof. Below him the courtyard was spread out. Firing was still coming from the tower. Carson and Kerr were still holding out.

His back pressed hard against the parapet, he watched McRee slowly approach. The blood-stained blade was resting casually on one shoulder. His eyes glowed sadistically as he carefully levelled the claymore on the trapped man's stomach.

'Die!' he roared and leapt forward in a final death-dealing lunge.

The night blasted open in a blaze of light. The darkness vanished. A gigantic fireball slowly descended over the castle.

The fighters were instantly blinded. It was too late for the Chief to stop his stroke, but the sword point wavered. The blade passed between Kennedy's chest and arm and the pommel crashed into his shoulder.

Without thought, he closed his arm on the blade trapping it. McRee's hot breath was on his face. Still blind, Kennedy swung round and off balance the Chief staggered to the parapet. It caught him behind the thighs. He teetered for a moment, then fell backwards into space. Kennedy listened as his scream followed him down. It still echoed from the courtyard after he was dead.

The journalist blinked rapidly until his vision cleared. Out in the waters of the loch the frigate lay at anchor. Tiny black dots of assault craft shot out white wakes as they carried men ashore. The ship's 4.5-inch gun leapt and another star shell floated down from the sky.

16

Kennedy relaxed on top of the late Roderick McRee's bed. It was a plain, almost spartan room. It told nothing of the character of that evil, but yet remarkable man.

A young Naval doctor had just finished cleaning and dressing his wounds. 'That will hold you together until we get you to hospital, Mr Kennedy. That injection will help kill the pain.

'By the way, there is someone outside who wants to see you first. Then it is into a chopper for you, my lad, and off to the mainland.'

Kennedy's mouth dropped open as Sir Colin Forbes came into the room.

'You have done a wonderful job here, David. Mrs Armstrong and the others have told me everything, but now I want to hear it from you.'

Twenty minutes later he had finished recounting his experiences. 'That frigate was the most wonderful sight in my life. Did the fire bring it in?'

The tycoon looked puzzled for a moment or two. 'No. It wasn't that at all.'

Early that morning the warship had received a signal by lamp from a small vessel that refused to identify itself. The stranger claimed there was some serious trouble on the island. At first the Navy had thought that the small unknown vessel might be Russian — but the signal had been sent in Gaelic. Luckily there was a rating from South Uist onboard.

The captain had contacted the Ministry of Defence and it had escalated from there. He had been ordered to go in and investigate. When the warship had steamed into the loch it had found a good going war in progress.

Charlie Fraser had met the first landing party and explained the situation. The islanders had suffered no casualties and the sailors had found Kerr and Carson wounded but still very much alive.

The arrival of the Royal Navy had broken the spirit of McRee's men and they had surrendered quietly.

'But why are you here, sir?' mumbled Kennedy. 'And coming to think of it why didn't help arrive a long time ago. If it had some good men might still be alive.'

Sir Colin moved uncomfortably in his chair. 'Well I gave you the forty-eight hours' grace that you asked for before informing Chief Superintendent Macdonald about that attempt on your life and what you were up to. The man was furious. He immediately got on the phone to the police here and was told you had left for Glasgow.'

Kennedy stared at the roof and sighed. 'Macdonald did not speak to the local copper. McRee must have intercepted the call. Constable McKay was already in McRee's dungeons.'

'Yes, that was hard luck,' grunted Sir Colin. 'Anyway after another twelve hours and you had not appeared I put half the staff on the job of finding you. I must admit for a time I did think you were dead.

'Then early this morning the news desk got a tip that a warship had been diverted into Bargrennan for some reason or other. I put two and two together and flew up here at first light in my own plane. Bringing an editorial team, of course. This will make a great story.

'And you must admit I was right. It took an amateur to catch amateurs. Now I must get back to Glasgow.'

As the tycoon reached the door he turned. There was a twinkle in his eye. 'That very attractive Mrs Armstrong tells me she is the owner of the Inverawe Hotel. I took the liberty of telling her that you will need a room to convalesce after you get out of hospital. For at least a month.

'A fine girl. Wasted in widowhood.'

Kennedy stared at the closed door, his mind in a turmoil of confused thought. Finally he shook his head in dismay. He could make nothing of it. Most probably never would. It had been luck that had given him that first lead. And it was only with luck that he had survived.

He swung his legs out of bed and crossed shakily to the window. A bright afternoon sun beat down on the loch and small craft beetled round the sleek grey frigate.

There was a fine pair of German binoculars on the window-ledge. Easing his right arm out of its sling he lifted them clumsily and holding them to his eyes swept them up the coast until he found the airstrip. A black heap of tangled wreckage littered the white concrete.

The newspaper owner got out of a car and headed for his plane. He was accompanied by a big man who had his head bent forward as if listening intently. He was limping badly. Kennedy could see his boss smash his fist into the palm of his other hand as if emphasizing some major point.

Sir Colin clambered up the ladder and into the aircraft. The other fellow followed and turning at the entrance for a moment, looked back at the castle. Kennedy bit his lip in surprise — it was Carson!

Bewilderment flooded him. Sir Colin had said only a few minutes ago that the private detective was in hospital on the mainland. But he had been fit enough to climb up that ladder. What was he doing with the boss?

The old bastard was keeping something — a lot — from him. Firstly he could not accept that tale about Macdonald's being conned into thinking he had left the island. The copper was not that stupid. Then that bit about half the staff trying to trace his whereabouts. The first place they would have tried would have been Bargrennan — but it seemed they had ignored the island. Now this with Carson. Had he been a pawn in some plot of Sir Colin's?

He groaned — as usual he knew sweet damn all. What the hell — he was alive and finally that was all that mattered.

He swung the glasses over to Inverawe. Scores of townsfolk lined the front watching the activities of the Navy. Then he picked out a small figure standing apart and alone at the end of the pier . . . waiting.

The Naval doctor stuck his head into the room. 'Get back into bed. I don't want you bleeding all over my best stretcher that my sick-bay tiffies are bringing up. We will soon have you off this damned place.'

Kennedy gave him a sly smile. 'But I am coming back.'

The officer grinned back at him. 'I don't blame you. That girl from the hotel has been pestering the life out of me all day about your condition. Lucky man!'

And that was not the only thing he was coming back for. He had a feeling that he had been used and did not like it. And that was why he had not told Sir Colin everything.

Somewhere under the stones of that shattered tower at the south end of Bargrennan there was a large steel box. He doubted very much if it had been destroyed in the explosion.

Sir Colin had told him to take a month's convalescence. And that should just be about right to dig up all that beautiful American currency.

We do hope that you have enjoyed reading this large print book.

Did you know that all of our titles are available for purchase?

We publish a wide range of high quality large print books including:
**Romances, Mysteries, Classics
General Fiction
Non Fiction and Westerns**

Special interest titles available in large print are:
**The Little Oxford Dictionary
Music Book, Song Book
Hymn Book, Service Book**

Also available from us courtesy of Oxford University Press:
**Young Readers' Dictionary
(large print edition)
Young Readers' Thesaurus
(large print edition)**

For further information or a free brochure, please contact us at:
**Ulverscroft Large Print Books Ltd.,
The Green, Bradgate Road, Anstey,
Leicester, LE7 7FU, England.
Tel:** (00 44) **0116 236 4325**
Fax: (00 44) **0116 234 0205**

Other titles in the
Linford Mystery Library:

THE CLEOPATRA SYNDICATE

Sydney J. Bounds

Maurice Cole, the inventor of a mysterious new perfume, is found murdered. But his employer's only concern is to recover the stolen perfume . . . He hires Daniel Shield, head of I.C.E. — the Industrial Counter Espionage agency — who is aided by Barney Ryker and the beautiful Melody Gay. The trail leads them to Egypt, where Shield must find international criminal Suliman Kalif and recover the perfume before the Nile runs red with the blood of a Holy War.

DR. MORELLE TAKES A BOW

Ernest Dudley

Miss Frayle, no longer employed by psychiatrist and detective Dr. Morelle, now works as secretary to Hugo Coltman, head of a drama school. Endeavouring to entice her back, Dr. Morelle accepts an invitation to lecture at the school, only to become entangled in the sinister schemes that threaten the lives of students and teachers. After a brutal murder, tension mounts as Dr. Morelle and Miss Frayle find themselves targeted by the killer. Can Dr. Morelle's investigation be successfully concluded, and the murderer unmasked?

BURY BY NIGHT

Lorette Foley

As the seaside village of Gifford basks in the June sun, the peace is shattered when the body of Simon Connolly is discovered, buried in another person's grave. Who struck him down, and what has become of his fiancée, Lily Sullivan? Detective Inspector Moss Coen arrives from Dublin, with his assistant, to investigate. When two people die suddenly and violently, Geraldine Lovell — Connolly's former fiancée — becomes involved . . . The solution eventually becomes clear — but not before the Inspector's assistant, Finnbarr Raftery, comes close to a watery end.